MAR 23

NOT TALKING ABOUT **YOU**

NOT TALKING ABOUT YOU

KEVIN HERONJONES

James Lorimer & Company Ltd., Publishers
Toronto

James Lorimer & Company Ltd., Publishers acknowledges funding support from
the Ontario Arts Council (OAC), an agency of the Government of Ontario. We
acknowledge the support of the Canada Council for the Arts, which last year
invested $153 million to bring the arts to Canadians throughout the country. This
project has been made possible in part by the Government of Canada and with
the support of Ontario Creates.

Cover design: Tyler Cleroux
Cover image: Shutterstock

Library and Archives Canada Cataloguing in Publication

Title: Not talking about you / Kevin heronJones.
Names: HeronJones, Kevin, 1975- author.
Identifiers: Canadiana (print) 20220275386 | Canadiana (ebook) 20220275394 |
ISBN 9781459417076 (softcover) | ISBN 9781459417083 (hardcover) | ISBN
9781459417090 (EPUB)
Classification: LCC PS8615.I754 N68 2022 | DDC jC813/.6—dc23

Published by:
James Lorimer & Company
Ltd., Publishers
117 Peter Street, Suite 304
Toronto, ON, Canada
M5V 0M3
www.lorimer.ca

Distributed in Canada by:
Formac Lorimer Books
5502 Atlantic Street
Halifax, NS, Canada
B3H 1G4
www.formaclorimerbooks.ca

Distributed in the US by:
Lerner Publisher Services
241 1st Ave. N.
Minneapolis, MN, USA
55401
www.lernerbooks.com

Printed and bound in Canada.
Manufactured by Friesens in Altona, MB in August 2022.
Job #291902

CONTENTS

This novel is dedicated to my twelve-year-old son Tyce and all young athletes. Sometimes we make mistakes. It's okay, but we always have the opportunity to do better. So do better.

CHAPTER 1

It was Khalil's first day at his new school. He stood in the playground by himself, watching other kids being dropped off by parents, then running mindlessly to meet groups of friends who were catching up after summer break. Others ran straight to the field to play soccer and football or to run around crazily before the bell rang. Khalil was athletic and loved to play sports. His favourite was to run track, high jump and long jump, but he was really good at soccer too. He wanted to join the boys on the field but was too shy to throw himself in the game, so he just walked the pavement surrounding the school.

He stopped to watch some girls skipping Double Dutch. He was good at that, too. He would skip with his cousin Marcia and her friends whenever his parents took him along to visit Uncle Randy and Aunt Gem. He watched the girls' quick feet pitta-pat pitta-pat as they ducked into the revolving ropes in pairs. Khalil always imagined they were stepping into a time machine, and if they skipped fast enough, it would transport them into the past or even way out into space. He contemplated joining in with the girls. That would be more fun than just standing on the pavement waiting for school to begin.

A few steps over were kids playing handball. Khalil was the handball champion at his old school. His father had shown him ways to slap the ball backhanded and forehanded with speed and power. Once again, he was too timid to get in the game. A few yards away, he noticed the boys on the basketball court. It was just one basketball net, with at least ten to twelve boys playing. Khalil hadn't played much basketball. Not organized anyway. He shot around at Bible camp but wasn't very good at it, so normally he played tether ball or would sit on the sidelines while his older cousins would look like professionals; they dribbled the ball like it was connected to the jelly sticky hand toy they'd give the kids after Sunday School. Any time Khalil would try to bounce the ball, it would ricochet off his knees, then hit the wall. So he was happy to stay on the sidelines for basketball.

He walked closer to the game. He instantly recognized that the boys were playing American Twenty-One. Not the shooting game, but the one-on-one-on-one-on-one game. Some of his American cousins would call it Uptown. One player against the world is how Khalil would describe it. Literally, the player with the ball was being defended by everyone else on the court with no one to pass to. Like a pack of rabid wolves attacking a lonely lamb. The aim was to be the first to score twenty-one points (some kids would play to eleven to make it quicker).

Khalil watched the boys on the court play. Defenders crowded around the boy with the ball. They slapped and swiped and clawed at him as he attempted to dribble into the hurricane of bodies. It was a dangerous game. Khalil couldn't even see the boy with the ball any longer, as defenders surrounded him. From the eye of the storm, the boy tossed up a shot that clanged off the metal backboard before bouncing into the rim.

"Game!" the boy yelled, punching the sky triumphantly. He didn't seem bothered by the stream of blood trickling down his wrist as he celebrated his game-winning basket.

"Oh, you got lucky. I had you right there. My finger jus' grazed that shot on the way up," said one of the wolf-like defenders.

Examining the blood on his arm, the boy who made the shot said, "Looks like you grazed more than jus' the ball. Lookit this. You fouled me, guy!"

The boys all began to argue with each other when the school bell rang. Khalil shook his head as he headed towards the school side entrance. *Those guys are crazy. Playing football seems less dangerous,* Khalil thought, while joining the line of students forcing their way inside. Walking down the hallway, Khalil searched for his classroom. He was assigned to class 8-3. Bumping off bodies like a pinball, he finally found his class at the end of the hall. There were about twenty students sitting at desks when he walked in. The teacher was sitting at her desk, watching the last few kids filter into the room. There were a few empty desks in the front of the class and a couple near the back beside the window. Khalil went straight for the window seat. He liked looking out into the blue sky and watching airplanes as they passed. He thought that one day he'd like to become a pilot and fly people all over the world.

The teacher rose to her feet and slowly approached the chalkboard where her name was already written in bold block letters. Some of the in-class conversations faded away as students noticed her walking to the front, but there was still the murmur of a few groups who either didn't notice or didn't care that the teacher was getting started. Somehow, Khalil had neglected to read the name as he came into the class, as he was more preoccupied with observing the other students. *Ms. Kirkland,* he mouthed the name as she began to speak.

"Hello class, I'm —"

Suddenly Khalil felt a gust of air as a boy darted into the room. The chair at the desk nearest to him squealed when he plopped into it. It was the boy from the basketball court who took the last shot before the bell rang. Khalil took note of the red scratch mark on his wrist as confirmation. The boy ran a hand through his blond hair, slouched back in his seat and elevated his feet onto the dark brown basketball he brought with him. Khalil admired the silver initials scribbled onto the leather that read C.C. He liked the way the letters gleamed off the ball. No one could mistakenly take the ball and claim it was an accident.

"Glad you could join us, Mr. Campbell. I hope we aren't keeping you from anything important."

"Not at all, Ms. Kirkland," he replied while sitting up in his seat. "Please excuse me. I didn't mean to interrupt. Please continue."

"Why thank you, Cameron. I shall," Ms. Kirkland said with a hint of sarcasm. The classroom chuckled at the interaction as Ms. Kirkland continued her introduction.

"Yes. Okay, class, as you can see, my name is Ms. Kirkland. I was born in Winnipeg, Manitoba, but moved to Milton, Ontario when I began my teaching career. I've been teaching for five years and I love puppies. So now that you know a little about me. How about each of you tell me about yourselves. Let's start with Cameron since he was the first to make his presence known."

Cameron looked over at Khalil and rolled his eyes while smiling.

"Thank you, Ms. Kirkland. I'll take it from here," he said, standing up and talking into his fist as if he were holding a microphone. Students giggled as he continued, "As many of you already know, my name is Cameron Campbell. Basketball Champion. Milton born and raised. On the playground is how I spend most of my days. And I am basketball. I am basketball."

Cameron turned the invisible microphone towards Khalil. "Now, back to you in the studio with the weather we have …"

Khalil froze. He hadn't expected Cameron to put him on the spot like that.

"… uhhh. Muh, my, my name is Khalil? Khalil Harris. I'm new here. I used to live in Toronto. And … and I like airplanes. I want to be a pilot."

"Thank you, Mr. Campbell. Mr. Harris, welcome to Milton. It's a pleasure to meet you both. Next. Sitting in front of Khalil. Please, yes you, go ahead," said Ms. Kirkland.

Khalil let out a large breath as he leaned back in his chair. He turned to Cameron, looking at him like, "why would you do that to me?" Cameron smiled genuinely while nodding and threw up thumbs as if to say, "great job!"

Ms. Kirkland went through the rest of the class introductions, then spoke about her expectations for the school year before talking about their first assignment. "Class, our first assignment will be to pick a subject you are passionate about and write a song or a poem about it. I want you to work in pairs. You can pick a partner and let me know tomorrow. Anyone who needs help finding a partner, please come to my desk," Ms. Kirkland said.

"Can we write a rap?" Cameron shouted.

"Yes, yes, of course. A rap is a song and a poem, so definitely," Ms. Kirkland replied.

Cameron fist-pumped his red, scratched arm like he'd done after making the winning shot. The bell rang, and the students hustled to get their things together to move on to the next class.

"Hey, Airplane."

Khalil looked up strangely at Cameron while putting his books in his backpack, wondering who he was talking to.

"Ya, you Torono. Airplane," Cameron continued. "You wanna be partners? This assignment should be easy."

"Uh okay. Ya, I guess we can."

"Great. I got the perfect idea we can do. You like basketball?"

Khalil shrugged.

"Well, we can write a rhyme about basketball. Whatchu think Airplane?"

Still looking puzzled, Khalil replied, "Okay? But how would we do it?"

"Leave it to me. We'll get this done easy and have extra time to hang out, too."

CHAPTER 2

The next day, Cameron showed up to class with a sheet of paper tightly rolled and wedged behind his left ear. Looking peculiarly at Cameron, Khalil pointed at the white cylinder on his head.

"Hey, Cam. What is that?"

"Sup Airplane," Cameron said while grabbing the paper and unravelling it. "It's our assignment. You know, the song we're writing."

"You did it all yourself?!" Khalil said, shocked.

"Nah, nah. It's just our roadmap. Y'know, to help us along the way. Okay, check this out. My older brother was playing this song called 'Basketball' by an old-school rapper named Kurtis Blow. So, look. I found the lyrics online and printed a copy. We can use them. Like, change them up a little to be about us."

"Uhhh, I don't think so. Isn't that cheating? I've heard of kids who got expelled for copying. What's it called again? Ummm, ya, plagiarism," Khalil said.

"We got nothing to worry about. No thirteen-year-old is getting expelled. Maybe suspended, but anyway, we ain't copying it. We're rewriting it. Like a revision." Cameron raised his eyebrows up and down in a persuasive manner.

"A rewrite?" Khalil questioned.

"Ya bruh. We jus' gotta change up the words a bit," said Cameron.

"I think that's plagiarism. My parents would kill me if I get suspended."

"It's not. Trust me," Cameron pleaded.

"I dunno man."

"Jus' trust me. What do you think rappers do? They always remake songs. Nothing's new under the sun. They take an old song like rock or R&B and remix to a rap song. We doing the same thing 'cept that we taking an old rap song and making a new rap song out of it."

"We can do that?" said Khalil.

"Of course we can. If anyone of us two should know that, it should be you. Ain't that what you guys do?" said Cameron.

Khalil wasn't sure if he heard correctly. "Huh? You guys ... what? I'm ... I'm not a rapper."

"Not yet. But you can obviously rap. I'm sure you're better at it than me. So look, this is what we do. We change up a word here and a word there and make it relevant to us ..."

As Cameron explained, Khalil was in his own thoughts. Wondering why Cameron assumed he was good at rapping.

Khalil had never even tried to rap before. He liked rap music, but never even thought to try doing it himself.

"... so ya, you see it's just that easy. See what I'm saying. Airplane? Yo! Airplane. You hear anything I just said?"

Khalil was jarred out of his thoughts. "Huh. Umm, ya okay. That's cool. We can do that."

The boys worked on their project, rearranging and rewriting the lyrics until they became somewhat original to them.

Yeah, now basketball is my favourite sport
I like when the girls see me dribble down the court
I got so much style when the game is on
You can call me a KING like the mighty LeBron
I wish I could slam dunk the ball in the hoop
Or like Zion Williamson catch the alley-oop
I pick-and-roll, run back door, give-and-go
I love that basketball c'mon everybody let's gooooo!!!
They call me Cammy Cam. And yo I'm Airplane
Together ain't no one can beat us in this game
Ugghhh!!! Huh huhhuh ha! To the hoop y'all

"So Cam, what's with all the grunting at the end? Like, is that really necessary?"

"Of course it is, bro. That's 'ol' skool.' Gotta give that Huh Ha! Trust me, it makes it better."

Khalil shook his head, laughing. "Well, if you say so, man. So I guess we're done now?"

"Ya, that's it. That was easy, right? Lemme jus' ask Miss."

Cameron snatched the paper with the lyrics off the desk and headed over to Ms. Kirkland.

"Hey, Miss. I think we're done. We finished writing our song," Cameron said, waving the sheet of paper in her direction.

"Okay Cameron, let me have a look."

Ms. Kirkland scanned over the page and gave it back to Cameron. "Okay, well done. Cameron go have a seat. I'm going to tell the class what phase two of the project will be."

Cameron walked back to his seat with a triumphant smile on his face and thumbs up aimed toward Khalil. Ms. Kirkland stood up to address the class.

"All right, class, how many of you have finished or are close to finishing the assignment?"

Most of the class threw their hands in the air.

"Great. I look forward to hearing them all soon."

A low began murmur began as the students looked around at each other confused.

"Hear them, Miss?" said Cameron.

"Yes, yes. This was part of my surprise. Phase two of our assignment will be to perform your song or poem at the school assembly next week." The students all gasped. Mostly out of nervousness. "So once your writing is complete, work on your delivery. Find music that you can perform to. I have a few links to instrumentals that you can use for this project. Or if you prefer, you can choose to go a cappella as well."

"What if we can't sing, Ms. Kirkland?" asked one of the students.

"Don't worry about it. Just do your best. Singing is just holding a note for an extended time. Every one of you is capable of that. I've heard you during class."

Khalil gulped and looked at Cameron, who looked surprised by the news but not nearly as nervous as the other kids in the class.

"Hear that Airplane? We get to hear you rap now. This should be exciting."

"But — but I can't rap."

"Sure you can. You're Black. Of course you can rap. I'm the one who should be worried. I'm white. Hahaha. How many good white rappers are out there?"

"That's just a stereotype. There's a ton of good white rappers."

"Ya and there's ten times more, better famous Black ones."

Although Khalil wanted to disagree, he couldn't. He didn't like the idea of being pegged into a stereotype, but he knew Cameron was correct in this case.

"Well, whatever man. I still can't rap, anyway."

"Don't be so down on yourself, bro. I bet you're much better than you give yourself credit for. You're jus' acting shy. Trust me. After a little practice. You'll be fine."

Khalil shrugged his shoulders.

"So look, let's do it like this," Cameron said. "I'll do the first line, then you say the next. And we'll go back and forth like that for the whole song. I saw a video of Run-DMC and that's how they did it. The ol' skool way. Sounds good?"

Again, Khalil shrugged. The boys got to work rehearsing the lines for the rest of the class.

CHAPTER 3

At lunch break, Khalil walked around the school, rehearsing his lines for the assignment. He was having trouble remembering which lines were his and which were Cameron's. He soon realized he'd have to memorize the whole song as if he were going to perform all the lyrics himself. He began to get frustrated because he couldn't keep the flow going as smooth as he knew it should sound. Trying to remember the next lyric threw off his rhythm, making the song sound choppy, like he was stuttering more than rapping.

He decided he would just head out to the field and play football or soccer; whatever game other kids were playing. He walked by the girls skipping before noticing the game of handball beside them. Khalil thought that maybe he should get in that game. He watched for a few minutes as the boys clapped at the blue and orange tennis ball they were playing with. The competitor in Khalil quickly emerged as he compared his abilities to the boys in the game. He knew he could beat them, so he walked closer to the crowd that semi-circled the match.

"Hey, Airplane! Yo. Airplane over here!"

Khalil heard the familiar voice but didn't see where it was coming from until he looked towards the basketball court. Cameron was waving him over.

"Over here, Khalil. Come!"

For the moment, Khalil abandoned his idea of getting in the handball game and jogged over to the basketball court.

"Hey, Cameron. Whassup."

"Yo. Get in the game with us. Wanna play?"

"I don't really play basketball."

"What! That's impossible. Of course you play basketball. Look at you. You have the perfect basketball physique. Look, we just need one more guy so we can play four on four. One of the guys jammed his finger so we need a replacement. C'mon, you'll be on my team."

Khalil looked over at the boy nursing his swollen pinky finger, debating if he should turn down Cameron and head back over to the handball wall, but Cameron was persistent.

"Come on, yo. It'll be fun. If you don't like it, then I'll never ask you again."

Khalil agreed with a soft head nod.

"Okay cool. So it's you, me, that guy, Blake, in the red shorts there and Dylan, with the Blue Jays hat turned backwards. Score is eight to five for the other team. Game is eleven. Ready?"

Khalil shrugged and nodded his head to say okay.

"Cool, let's go!" Cameron yelled, dribbling the ball to the top of the key while pointing out instructions. "Dylan, Blake, you guys take the wings. One on the left, ya like that, and the other one on the right. Yo, Airplane, you go down low. Stand down there close to the basket. No, no, go deeper. Keep going. Okay, perfect. Now, when a shot goes up, you grab the rebound. If we pass it to you, shoot the ball. Alright! Check."

Cameron bounced the ball to the defender in front of him. The defender caught the ball and casually looked behind him on either side to make sure his teammates were set on defence. Satisfied with everyone's position, he bounced the ball back to Cameron. "Check!" he yelled while dropping into his defensive stance.

Cameron caught the pumpkin and slapped it twice before crouching into a triple threat position; right foot forward and centre of gravity low. He leaned headfirst, securing the ball close to his left hip in both palms, away from the swiping hands of his defender. Khalil watched as Cameron jab stepped and pump faked the defender, trying to get him off balance. Khalil had a flashback of a basketball video he watched. In it they explained players would duck into triple threat position because it makes them ready to shoot, pass or dribble the ball, and the defence would have no idea which moves you plan to make.

Instinctively, Khalil fought for position, keeping the defender on his back as he raised his hand and called to Cameron to pass him the ball. Cameron faked the shot and his defender jumped off his feet. Cameron drove by him and the other two defenders collapsed to the middle to stop the ball. Seeing this, Cameron smartly passed the ball out to Dylan on the wing, who caught the pass and drained the jumper.

Again, Cameron checked the ball and went through his triple threat routine. He scored himself this time. After that, he hooked up Blake for a score. Khalil was beginning to feel like a human pylon.

He wondered why he was fighting so much under the rim if he wasn't getting a chance to touch the ball. Even though he didn't really want to play in the first place and was doing Cameron a favour by standing in, his competitive juices were beginning to flow.

This time, when Cameron checked the ball, Khalil jumped up and down repeatedly, waving his hands to get Cameron's attention.

"He ain't gonna pass to the new guy!" yelled Navdeep, who was defending the ball. Cameron looked off Khalil wanting to pass to Blake, but Blake was covered. Cameron looked in Dylan's direction, but Dylan couldn't shake his defender, either. Cameron tried to drive to the rim himself, but Khalil's defender stepped up and double-teamed him, forcing Cameron to pick up his dribble.

"Steal! Grab the ball now!" yelled Navdeep.

With everyone else covered, Cameron had no choice but to lob a high pass to the open Khalil. Khalil jumped and grabbed the ball in the air, excited that he was finally getting involved in the game. Now that he had the ball, he realized that he never thought about what he was going to do with it. He stood tall, raised the ball above his head, his arms stretched out toward the sky and turned toward the rim. The opposing defenders all collapsed on him, slapping at his wrists and elbows, trying to whack the ball loose. Khalil figured he should try to shoot, but he couldn't see the rim clearly with the defenders crowding him and suddenly dropped the ball. At the same time, Cameron yelled, "FOUL! FOUL! C'mon, check it back to the top. You guys are mugging him."

"That's no foul!" Navdeep yelled back, approaching Cameron.

"You're always fouling, Naaaavdipstick!" Blake shouted. "Can't play defence, so you just slap all over the place. Look how red my arms are from your so-called defence."

"Oh puhleeeze!" Navdeep replied while pulling up his sleeve. "You're the one who's always slappin'. Think all these scratches came from nowhere? I ain't got no cat. Cut your fingernails once in a while!"

Blake advanced toward Navdeep until their noses were nearly touching. "You gotta problem with me. What if I take these nails and scratch your eyes out?"

"I'd like to see you try!" Navdeep said, pushing Blake out of his personal space. Blake pounced at Navdeep but was held back by Dylan and Cameron. The boys on the other team were holding back Navdeep.

"Chill. Okay guys, chill. Let's jus' finish this before the bell rings!" shouted Cameron. The boys began to relax. Navdeep walked by Khalil and whispered to him, "Hey, New Guy. Maybe you don't know it now, but you're on the wrong team, bro."

Khalil was taken aback by the comment. He didn't know anyone there well enough to know what Navdeep was talking about, so he shrugged it off. Blake and Navdeep scowled at each other as the boys reset themselves to check the ball again. Cameron walked over to Khalil and patted him on the shoulder while laughing. "Nice job, Airplane. Hahaha. Next time shoot the ball or pass it to one of us. Okay? Okay."

Khalil nodded, and they all got into place. He was determined to score the next time he got a chance to touch the ball.

"Yo, what's the score?" one boy yelled.

"Tied at eight. First to score three points wins," Cameron yelled back while caressing the ball. "Okay, ball in!"

Cameron checked the ball to the defender and dropped into his three-point stance. He passed the ball to Blake, who passed it to Dylan, who passed it back to Cameron, then back to Dylan again, who scored from the baseline. Khalil shuffled from one side of the key to the opposite side as the boys passed the ball to each other around the horn. He didn't understand why no one would pass him the ball and was getting frustrated. He felt like he was playing monkey in the middle. He wondered why they even bothered to ask him to play if they weren't going to include him in the offense. It continued this way with each team scoring twice.

"Game point!" Cameron yelled as he took the ball at the top of the key. "Tied at ten. Next point wins."

"Thought we were playing win by two," Navdeep hollered.

"Nah. Not enough time. Recess almost over," Cameron replied. "We playing to eleven straight."

They checked the ball and again Khalil shuffled side to

side and watching his teammates pass to each other and not to him. Fed up, he just stopped moving until Blake threw up a wild shot with a defender right in his face. Khalil realized this was his opportunity to finally get involved. The ball clanked off the side of the backboard. Khalil wrestled by his defender and jumped as high as he could. Two boys for the opposing team also jumped, but Khalil skied high above their heads. He caught the ball and in one motion put up the shot same time as if he had caught an alley-oop pass. The ball kissed the backboard and dropped through the net. All the boys stood in awe and disbelief that Khalil was able to make such a spectacular play.

"That's game!" Cameron yelled while jumping onto Khalil's back. "You did it! You did it! We won!" Blake and Dylan excitedly joined the celebration, cheering him on, patting Khalil on his back and high-fiving each other.

"Bro. How did you do that?" Dylan said.

"Ya dude, that was amazing!" Blake added. "After I missed so badly, I thought for sure we were gonna lose. You got some hops dude! You were jus' hanging in the air waiting for the ball to come down."

Cameron grabbed Khalil's wrist and hoisted his arm into the air, yelling, "The champ is here! The champ is here! Ya, Airplane, it was like you were flying. Like ... like an airplane, bro. Hahahahaha." Cameron pounded his chest. "Hey, and I brought him here guys. Me. I did that. I'm like his manager or his agent, so back off guys, let my client speak."

Cameron held his fist close to Khalil's face, pretending it was a microphone. "Go ahead, Airplane. Tell the people how you did it."

Khalil shrugged, wondering why Cameron was trying to take credit when he didn't even want to pass Khalil the ball in the first place. None of the guys did, and now they were praising him. He chuckled at the irony. Khalil looked down at Cameron's fist and swiped the pretend microphone out of his face.

"No comment. Next question," Khalil said jokingly as if he were an agitated athlete talking to the press. All the boys exploded with laughter and pounded fists with Khalil for the clever response.

CHAPTER 4

After just one week of playing with Cameron and the guys, Khalil saw great improvement with his game. He played with them every recess and lunch break and was learning the nuances of the game quickly. He was still getting accustomed to the rules and strategy, but he was advanced with the physical aspects of the game. He was stronger, could run faster and jump higher than all the boys he was playing with. He was dominant on defence, blocking shots and grabbing rebounds like a real player.

"You're a beast!" Cameron said after Khalil ripped down a rebound during a game at first recess. "The way you grab that ball is like an animal. Maybe we have to stop calling you Airplane and start calling you something like Air-ape or Air-gorilla."

All the boys laughed. Some a little too hard for Khalil's

comfort. Still, Khalil chuckled with them anyway, a little awkwardly not revealing how uneasy he felt with the ape description. The bell rang to go back to class. As the other kids were migrating to the doors, Cameron gathered his boys together.

"Hey Blake, Dyl ... lunchtime, my house, okay?"

"Ya, for sure," said Dylan. Blake chimed in next. "Ya. No doubt. We playing or are we eating. You know I gotta eat."

"Hahaha. Ya bro, we eating and balling, don't worry," Cameron said.

Dylan and Blake dapped hands with Cameron, then with Khalil, and made their way into the school. Cameron and Khalil followed.

"You coming to my house too, right?" Cameron said to Khalil.

"Ummm. I guess. Wha ... whatchu guys doin'?"

"We gonna hoop. My mom will make us lunch while we play."

"I brought my lunch and my folks won't know I'm leaving school premises. I don't think they'll like that. Especially if we're late. Are we gonna make it back in time? Remember, we have to do the performance for Ms. Kirkland after lunch."

"Uhhhh. Airplane, you worry too much. The performance will be fine. We're never late. I live close. Only two minutes away. And you can bring your lunch, eat it at my house. You can even have your lunch and my mother's lunch if you want. Jus' be cool, man. Come. We need four to play two-on-two. So you gotta come."

"Well ... okay, I guess. As long as we get back on time."

"Ya dude. Don't worry. We good," Cameron said while playfully jabbing Khalil in the ribs. Khalil winced as if he were in pain as they walked through the doors of the school.

At lunchtime, kids raced out of the school doors. Cameron and Khalil met Blake and Dylan out on the soccer field.

"Guys ready?" Cameron said.

They all nodded.

"Cool, let's go! Last one there has to smell my brother's sneakers."

They took off before Khalil could register what was happening. Khalil was thinking about how putrid the sneakers must be if that was the punishment. When he saw how far up ahead the other boys were, he sprinted to catch up, holding his lunch bag away from his body so it wouldn't bounce off his legs as he ran. Khalil caught up quickly. He knew he could outrun the other boys, but he had no idea where he was running to, so he slowed his pace and jogged beside Cameron, who looked to have been running as fast as he could.

Khalil had yet to explore the neighbourhood around the school. As he ran, he couldn't help but notice how big and affluent the houses were. Everything was large and spacious. Tall trees with widespread branches and leaves that stretched over broad houses like giant green umbrellas. Khalil observed the well-manicured lawns and properties that he saw in the suburban real estate magazine his parents brought home last year. He'd daydreamed while flipping through the pages about one day being able to buy one of those homes for them after he became a pilot.

Little did Khalil know his parents were already planning to move to one of the neighbourhoods in the magazine. Khalil vowed now that he would buy them a mansion one day with enough land for a farm like the one his father grew up on. Ever since his family went on vacation last year to visit his grandparents in St. Vincent, Khalil had been obsessed with having chickens, cows and pigs. Every morning he would get up with his father and do chores like milking their cow, Shelly, and feeding all the animals. Khalil gave names to the nine chickens roaming the yard as he tossed them grains.

"I'd have to do this every morning before going to school, Khal. You're very lucky to grow up in Canada with all the luxuries I wish I had as a kid," his father would say. "But that's why we work hard. To give you a better life than we had."

Khalil never took it for granted and wanted to work hard like his father. He knew the difference between his middle-class life compared to his parents, who grew up with a lot less. Now his mother was a nurse and his father, a mining engineer. As Khalil inhaled the air of this new neighbourhood, he could hear his father saying, "Remember, work hard and you too could be successful in this country."

The boys jogged toward a street on the left, a mustard-coloured sign with black bold letters read NO EXIT. The other boys abruptly hung a left and began sprinting again. Not wanting to be last, Khalil picked up speed, still not knowing where the finish line was until he noticed the house straight ahead. The only one with a basketball hoop in the driveway. Khalil switched gears and darted towards the net, leaving the other boys in the dust. He reached the finish line, hands raised, feeling victorious; relieved he wouldn't have to sniff any smelly shoes. Bent over, trying to catch his breath, he watched Cameron lead the boys into the driveway next door. Khalil's heart sank as the boys pointed and laughed at him.

"You lose! You're sniffin' sneakers," they cackled. Khalil tried to protest until Cameron threw his arm over Khalil's shoulder.

"Just playin' man. You're in the right place. This is my house."

That's when Khalil realized that what he thought was a different house was actually all the same property. Cameron's three-door garage in front of the basketball hoop looked like a mini residence as if the cars had their own home. Thankful, he leaned against the pole. Still breathing heavily, he noticed the pole for the basketball net was embedded in the cement driveway, like at the park or at school; unlike the portable nets on wheels he was accustomed to seeing at most houses. Cameron dashed to the side of the garage and disappeared through a side door. He re-emerged holding a basketball and tossed it at Blake.

"You guys warm up. I'm gonna let Mom know we're here," Cameron yelled, then took off towards the bigger house. Familiar with the routine, Blake and Dylan began putting up shots. Khalil joined in. As he took his first shot, Khalil watched the ball arc under the leaves of the trees that surrounded Cameron's home. To Khalil, it was as if they were playing in a green dome. There was so much shade because of the foliage it felt like it was evening. But the sun would occasionally poke through the green roof to remind him it was midday.

Cameron soon returned wearing a broad white headband, strands from his golden mane hung over the top of it. He flicked his bangs back saying, "Alright boys. Mom's gonna call us when lunch is ready. Let's go two-on-two. Me and Airplane against you guys."

Blake and Dylan nodded, then moved into position on the court. "We get first," Dylan said, passing the ball to Cameron from the spot on the driveway that would be top of the key. Since there were no lines drawn on the driveway, they estimated where the lines would be.

"Game on!" Dylan yelled, making a pass to Blake. Cameron and Khalil won two out of the three games they played before Cameron's mother hollered at them from the kitchen window. The boys rushed into the house. When Khalil entered, he began to take off his shoes but realized the other boys had neglected to do so. Cameron's mother greeted the boys as they entered and introduced herself to Khalil.

"You must be Airplane. Hello, I'm Cam's mother. Welcome. Leave your shoes on honey. The washroom is right over there, where the boys are. You can go wash up and meet them at the table. You like hotdogs?"

Khalil nodded enthusiastically while holding his bagged lunch high as if to say sorry that he had brought it with him. Cameron's mother smiled endearingly and said, "Eat your lunch. It's okay. I know your mother took the time to prepare it, so you better eat it. Then, if you still have room, you definitely can have a hotdog, too. That sound good to you?"

Khalil nodded again, happy that he didn't have to choose

between his lunch and Cameron's mother's lunch. He went to wash up and, as he was heading toward the kitchen, he heard a high-pitched pulsing beep. He saw the boys rushing towards the microwave, each pulling out hotdogs and buns individually wrapped in paper towel. Cameron saw Khalil approaching. "Hey Airplane, other way. Turn around, we goin' to the TV room."

CHAPTER 5

The boys hurried past Khalil into a room with a movie screen on the wall. They plunked onto the sectional sofas arranged in an open rectangle facing the screen for perfect movie viewing. The room had theatre lighting, and the ceiling was a night sky full of stars looking as if taken from the planetarium. The boys greedily unwrapped their lunches while Khalil tried to decide where to sit.

"Yo Plane, right here. Sit," Cameron said, pointing to a spot on the couch near to where he sat. "And here, I brought a hotdog for you too." Khalil took the mummy-wrapped hotdog, sat down and took out his lunch. He was amazed that microwave hotdogs could smell so good. It made his mouth water. He'd never had a microwaved hotdog before. His family usually boiled theirs. He would often peer into the pot at the dogs bathing in bubbles while holding his nose because he hated the smell of drowning meat.

To top it off, each steaming microwave dog was smothered with melted cheese. Another thing he never thought to do before. Khalil took out his sandwich, mashed corned beef on hard dough bread from the Caribbean grocery store. Although he liked corned beef, he was already craving that hotdog Cameron gave him. Khalil quickly ate half the sandwich, stuffed the rest back into the bag, and unwrapped his hotdog. He gobbled it down just as quickly, as the other boys had theirs, and was ready for more. All the boys were, so Cameron darted back to the kitchen to let his mother know. He came back shortly with another tray full of the mummified cuisine.

"Oh ya. Was so hungry, almost forgot to put the TV on," Cameron said as he dropped the tray down on the sofa and reached for the remote. The projector screen lit up as Cameron flipped through channels to YouTube TV and clicked it on. Khalil felt as if he were at the movies. Normally, he would have to go on his tablet to access YouTube. Here they could just watch it on TV. The boys watched basketball highlights while finishing their lunch. LeBron James, Kyrie Irving, Kevin Durant and Steph Curry entertained the boys with circus shots, fancy passes and flashy dribbling.

"See that. We gotta have handles like Kyrie for the upcoming season. Tryouts are coming soon. Airplane, you gonna tryout too, right?"

Khalil shrugged. "I guess. Uh ya. I'll try out with you guys ... ummmm what are handles?"

The three other boys looked at each other in disbelief and started laughing.

"Dude!" Blake yelled. "You're joking, right? Like, isn't that part of you guys' slang?"

"You guys?" Khalil questioned.

"Ya, y'know like Black guys. Like, ain't that part of the way you guys talk?"

Khalil felt himself getting uncomfortable; stomach fluttering as if he had swallowed a dragonfly. A combination of anger and confusion prickled his skin like pine needles. "Look I don't know. Not every Black person speaks the same. Besides, I don't speak slang. My parents don't like it. At home, we have to speak proper English. And are you sure that's Black talk or is it basketball talk? Because as you know, I'm just learning to play. So I obviously wouldn't know everything about it."

The boys were silent as Khalil reached into his lunch bag to pull out his desert, a small tan-coloured cake with a rough surface resembling a rock. The boys looked curiously at Khalil as he took a bite and tan bits crumbled to his lap.

"What's that?" Cameron asked.

"My mother made it. It's called a rock cake."

"Gimme some. Lemme taste. It looks like a muffin," said Cameron.

Khalil gave Cameron a piece and held the rock cake out to Dylan and Blake. They each took a piece. Blake was first to slowly bite into it.

"Arhhh," Blake hollered. Cameron followed with a choking cough. Khalil and Dylan looked at one another.

"Wha ... what's wrong?" Dylan said.

"Oh my god. Like I almost broke my tooth," Blake said, laughing hysterically.

Cameron was laughing and choking at the same time. "That really is a rock," Cameron said while knocking the cake against the wall. Blake did the same, reaching above his head to the wall behind him, and they both laughed even harder.

"It's not that hard," Khalil protested. "Just the outside."

Dylan still held his piece and looked at the others for some direction.

"Don't do it, Dyl. Trust me. Don't ..." Blake said, shaking his head and waving his hands, now trying to contain his laughter.

"Not if you value your teeth," Cameron joined in. They burst out laughing again.

Dylan saw the distraught look on Khalil's face and cautiously took a bite. He looked up at the ceiling as he chewed. "Is that ... is that coconut?"

Khalil's face brightened. "Yes. Yes, it is. My mom makes them with coconut and nutmeg and other stuff."

"Ya, it's good. I like it."

"You want mine?" Blake quickly offered.

"For sure," Dylan said. "Give it here."

"Heads up," Blake said, winding up and pitching the rock cake at Dylan as if it were a baseball.

Cameron took a pretend bite as if biting the pin out of a grenade, and turned to Dylan, "Take mine too," then tossed it, arm fully extended, yelling, "FIRE IN THE HOLE!!!"

Both he and Blake plugged their ears with their fingers as Dylan grabbed the rock cake out of the air. "Hahaha. Stop guys, it's not that bad. It's soft on the inside. And it tastes good too," said Dylan.

Khalil shook his head, disappointed with how Cameron and Blake were clowning one of his favourite Caribbean treats. It's one thing to not like it, but Khalil was infuriated with the way they were acting. Still, he tried to play it off as if it didn't bother him as much as it did.

"Don't listen to these fools," Dylan said. "I like it. The next time you bring one, I definitely want some again."

Khalil appreciated what Dylan said and decided to let go of the tightness he was feeling because of Blake and Cameron. He didn't care so much about Blake's response since he didn't know him well enough, but he just didn't expect Cameron to act that way, too.

CHAPTER 6

The boys headed back to school after lunch. This time, they walked while debating who the best NBA players were. Cameron and Blake said it was LeBron, "hands down." Dylan campaigned for KD. He argued that Kevin Durant was unstoppable. "A seven-footer with ball-handling skills who could shoot from anywhere. Who could beat that?"

Khalil wasn't sure. He didn't watch a lot of basketball, but he knew it was hard to dispute what the other boys were saying. "What about Steph Curry or the Beard James Harden or Giannis Antetokounmpo? Maybe LeBron is too old to still be the best?" said Khalil.

"Ya, good point," said Dylan. "They all have been MVPs. I'm still Team KD, but ya, they up there too. Like top five at least."

"True, true," Cameron said. "I like Steph. Maybe Harden. But Giannis can't shoot."

Blake started giggling to himself before spouting out, "Anteto-poopoo. Poopoo. Anteto-poopoo."

Blake and Cameron burst out laughing as if it was the funniest thing in the world. Dylan and Khalil chuckled, but nothing close to the gut-busting laughter from the other two boys. As they turned onto the next street, Cameron yelled, "Oh ya. Arnold Chen's rim! C'mon quick."

He ran over, dribbling the dark brown basketball that he carried with him. They all followed Cameron to a house with an old-looking basketball net in the driveway with a wooden pole. The hoop was shorter than the regulation ten feet that most rims were. This hoop was only seven feet high. Low enough to dunk. Cameron dribbled as fast as he could and jumped. He floated above the rim, cocking the ball behind his head with both hands, and slammed it as hard as he could through the hoop. He growled as he hung on the rim, legs swinging high, almost touching the backboard.

"Whooooooooaaaaahhhhh!!!" the boys wailed.

"Me next, me next," yelled Blake. Ball in hand, he took off like running down a runway with no dribbles and launched himself from a chalk mark that was supposed to be the free-throw line. He sailed to the rim with the ball in one hand high above his head. When he got to the hoop, he tried to punish the rim by slamming it as hard as he could. The ball hit the back of the rim and rebounded high in the air back to where Blake had originally started running.

"That looked amazing!" Cameron shouted. "You missed,

but it still looked crazy!" Dylan was next. He did a double pump two-handed dunk from the baseline. Cameron tossed the ball to Khalil. "Alright, Airplane, you're next. Let's see if you can live up to the nickname."

Khalil caught the ball and thought about what he could do. He had no idea. Then he thought if they should even be dunking on this rim at all since it belonged to someone else.

"Hey Cam," Dylan said. "What about Arnold?"

"What about him?"

"Is he here?"

"I dunno. He's probably at school already."

"Sooo, should we be playing here? I mean, like without him?"

It was as if Dylan could read Khalil's mind because he was thinking the exact same thing. Khalil nodded repeatedly and said, "We're not gonna get into trouble for playing here, are we? What if his parents come home?"

"Oh, it's cool. Arnold said I could play here anytime. Don't sweat it. Now dunk the darn ball. C'mon, do anything. If we could dunk on this, so can you."

Khalil thought about a dunk he saw at Cameron's place. A throwback dunk by Vince Carter. Khalil dribbled slowly and propelled himself towards the rim with the ball in both hands. He had no idea if he could actually complete the dunk, but he flew with determination. As he rose higher and higher, he brought the ball down to his waist in a circular motion, then completed the circle with a one-handed cram through the net. His momentum propelled him backwards dropping him on his backside beside the basketball pole.

"WHHOOOOAAA! A windmill," the boys declared.

They ran over to pick Khalil off the ground.

"Do you know what you just did!" exclaimed Cameron. Still disoriented from the fall, Khalil squinted at the boys who had surrounded him in celebration. He wasn't even sure he had made the dunk until they told him.

"How did you do that?" Dylan said.

"I dunno. I just thought I'd try something we saw on the highlights earlier."

"That was dope," Cameron said.

"Ya, I gotta admit, that looked really cool," said Blake.

They all high-fived Khalil then continued to try the craziest, most difficult dunks they had watched on highlights. Khalil felt like a real NBA player on this low rim. Like he was making highlights. The boys' excitement was on supercharge as each completed reverse dunks, Tomahawk dunks, leaners and anything they could think of. They chanted and screamed in celebration with each dunk attempt, make or miss. As Dylan was trying a between-the-legs dunk, Khalil noticed a woman watching them from the window of the house.

"Hey, I think Arnold's mother is home. I think she's staring at us. Maybe we shouldn't be here," said Khalil.

She disappeared suddenly when all the boys looked towards the window.

"I think his mother works. That might be his grandmother. What did she look like? Did she look old?"

"Not sure. Couldn't get a good look at her."

"Did she look like this?"

Cameron pulled on the outside of each eyelid until his

eyes took on an almond shape. Blake did the same, but much more exaggerated until his eyes became thin slits. They laughed at each other, prancing about while making noises you would hear in a martial arts movie.

Khalil dropped his jaw in shock. He knew something had to be wrong with what he was seeing.

"Uhhh, maybe we should go, guys. We don't want to be late," Khalil said.

"Don't worry. We're good. We're never late," said Cameron. "Jus' one more alley-oop. Blake, toss it up for me. I'm gonna rip this rim down!"

Blake threw the ball towards the rim; as Cameron leaped up to meet it, the front door swung open. An elderly woman stood on the porch in a shiny aqua-coloured robe, waving a long-handled wooden spoon, and yelling at the boys in a language they couldn't understand. Startled, the boys took off immediately and didn't stop until they neared the school playground. The boys slowed their pace, catching their breath. Khalil and Dylan were up ahead, still walking fast, but Blake and Cameron seemed to be taking their time.

"We better not be late," Khalil said, turning to Dylan.

"I think we'll be okay. We go to Cam's house at least once a week and we usually make it back on time."

"Usually?"

"Ya, except when Cam is losing and wants to keep going until he wins. Sometimes he's a sore loser. Flips out then curses everyone out."

"Oh ..." Khalil said with a look of concern.

"Don't get me wrong. Cam's a cool guy. We have a lot of

fun and joke around all the time. I've known him forever. Been on the same hockey and baseball teams for years. Our families are close. So we're kinda like brothers."

"Ya, I know he's cool. He's a comedian, makes me laugh in class. You're pretty quiet compared to him." Khalil peeked behind at Cameron and Blake, then lowered his voice to a whisper. "And you don't act like a jackass when Blake's around like he does."

"Hahahahaha. Airplane, you're pretty funny. Ah, they get kinda crazy when they're together. Don't let Blake bother you. He can be a clown at times. But both of them are good friends. We look out for each other."

"So what was that at Arnold's house? Like I don't think they should be mimicking Chinese people like that."

"They were just foolin' around. I don't think they meant anything by it."

"But you didn't do it with them. How come?"

"I dunno. I guess ... guess cuz I wouldn't feel comfortable doin' it?" Dylan said as they reached the school. The boys gasped when they saw that the playground was empty. They sprinted to the doors and ran into the school. Dylan and Blake went their separate ways while Khalil and Cameron darted to their homeroom. They peeked into the class and saw their classmates talking casually amongst themselves. Ms. Kirkland wasn't at her desk. Relieved, they nonchalantly headed to their desks and sat down.

"Whew, that was a close one," Cameron said.

"I know, I know. We got lucky," said Khalil.

"Okay, so let's practice this rhyme," said Cameron.

They rehearsed the lines for their rap song to perform

during class. Khalil just wanted to get the whole performance over with. He wasn't confident at all in his ability to rap. As he practiced, he knew he was off beat and lacked rhythm. But Cameron continued to encourage him. Khalil liked this version of Cameron much more than the one who threw rock cakes like grenades and mimicked Arnold Chen's grandmother.

Just then, the class went silent. Ms. Kirkland came through the door holding a stack of papers. She walked in the direction of the two boys, then turned toward her desk.

The boys looked at each other and grinned before Ms. Kirkland turned back around to face them.

"You boys are LATE!"

CHAPTER 7

For arriving late from lunch, Ms. Kirkland awarded the boys an all-expense-paid vacation to detention for the last recess. Ms. Kirkland worked on her laptop while the boys sat with their heads down. The rest of the class was empty except for those three. Khalil was nervous, hoping he wouldn't be in too much trouble with his parents for being punished at school. He was thinking of what to say to his parents when Ms. Kirkland approached their desks.

"Hello, boys. It's not nap time. This is not daycare. Sit up. Please sit up."

The boys raised their heads reluctantly as Ms. Kirkland continued.

"I already spoke to you about the importance of being on time during class, so this is your last chance. Next time, I tell your parents. I think you are good boys, and you know better. So I trust this will not happen again, right?"

The boys quickly nodded, affirming that they understood.

"Great. So, what I want to talk to you about was your performance during class earlier. Now I must say, I was very impressed with how you boys did. I really like the song you wrote, and you had one of the better performances in the class."

Khalil looked over at Cameron, surprised. Cameron smiled confidently, raising his eyebrows as if to say, "See, I told you."

"However, I think you can make it better for the assembly tomorrow. Whenever I see rap videos, the guys look like they're having more fun. You boys look stiff. Khalil, loosen up a little bit. I know you might be nervous, but when I see the rap guys, they move around. They talk with their hands. They smile with diamond teeth or they scowl like this."

Khalil and Cameron giggled as they watched Ms. Kirkland making stink faces and waving her arms around like the tall balloon man outside the car dealership.

"They are very expressive. They have flavour. Flavour! I need to see more of that flavour in your performance. So go ahead, let me see what you got."

Cameron and Khalil started to recite the song, trying to exaggerate their expression like Ms. Kirkland said.

"That's it. More of that. Yes!" Ms. Kirkland said excitedly, clapping her hands together. "It's getting better. Do you have any props? Look, that basketball down there. One of you should hold it. And you should wear basketball gear.

Jerseys and sneakers. Right? Okay, keep practicing. I'll be over at my desk if you need anything."

Cameron picked up his ball and tossed it to Khalil. "Here. I got an idea. You should hold the basketball when you do your verse, then pass it to me when it's time to do mine. So whoever is rapping will hold the ball. And we could pass it fancy like Trey Young's no-look pass or fake it and then pass it behind the back, y'know. And we should dance too."

Khalil made an unsure face at the suggestion. "I don't dance. I mean, I can't dance ..."

"What? Get outta here. I'm the one who should be saying that. Not you, my dude. I'm white."

"Just because you're white? C'mon, that doesn't mean anything. Plenty of white people are good dancers."

"Ya, but it means that you could probably dance better than me. You're jus' nervous. I know how to at least two-step and bounce a bit. Like this," Cameron began making a beat with his mouth and stepping side to side."

"Okay, you're right. I take that back. You can't dance either," Khalil said, laughing. "You're dancing off beat and you're the one making the beat. Hahahahahaha."

"Aw shut up, bro," Cameron said, laughing with Khalil. "Okay, well then you go."

Cameron continued beat-boxing, urging Khalil to show his moves.

"Nope. Nah uh," said Khalil. "Not doing it. I'm not about to embarrass myself in front of all those people at the assembly. No way."

"Guy ... you heard teach. We gotta put more flaaaavaa in it," Cameron said.

The boys laughed, peeking over at Ms. Kirkland to see if she knew they were laughing at her.

"Okay, so look. We're gonna do the best performance out of the whole class. I promise you," Cameron said, punching his palm. "So, okay, maybe we don't dance. Say we just do basketball moves to the music. Y'know? Like, pretend you're dribbling on stage. Jump shots, layups, dunks. Make it real crazy so that there's a lot going on at the same time."

Khalil nodded his approval. "I like that. We can do some of those Arnold Chen's hoop dunks on stage."

"Exactly, bro. We can even have like a hoop on the stage and do the dunks." Cameron pretended to do a two-handed reverse dunk while flashing his teeth.

"Yah ya. I got a mini hoop on my closet door. I'll bring it! We could use that. But somebody has to hold it," said Khalil. He stroked his chin, trying to think of other things that might be useful for the performance.

"Cool ya. We can get Blake and Dylan to help us on stage," Cameron said. "We can pass the hoop around and take turns dunking during the performance. Do you have any basketball jerseys?"

"Nope. I might have an old NY Knicks T-shirt, but I doubt that it still fits," said Khalil.

"Okay, I got some extra jerseys and b-ball gear. I'll bring them for us to wear. Hey, and we should have our own handshake that we do on stage. Y'know like how all the best ballers do."

"Handshake? Okay, but they look so complicated. How should we do it?" Khalil was always amazed at how perfectly basketball players could do their handshakes. He never thought that he would have a chance to make up his own handshake routine because they looked so hard to do.

"We should start with — say, with three hand slaps, then three daps. Ummm next ..." Cameron began.

"We should do three backhand slaps too," said Khalil.

"Okay, ya that's good!" hollered Cameron.

"Then how about we connect thumbs and open our hands, so it looks like wings," said Khalil

"Huh?" This time Cameron was confused.

"I saw LeBron do it with another player like this." Khalil demonstrated the move with his own hands.

"Nice. I dig that. So when we do that, we should raise our hands up and down and wiggle our fingers at the same time, so it looks like our hands are flying."

"Next you should pretend to do a crossover dribble and I'll fall down like as if you broke my ankles." Khalil pretended to lose his balance and trip over his feet, falling to the floor like a defender trying to cover Ja Morant.

"Yes, yes, that will be hilarious," Cameron said, laughing. "Then when you get up, we'll both throw our hands in the air and do a hop. Then to end it, maybe we should slide or something?"

"No, no, we should end it with kung fu fighting and do a kung fu bow!" Khalil held his hands up in fighting position.

"Wow, ya. That's it."

"That's a lot to remember. We gotta practice it," said Khalil.

"Ya, for sure," Cameron replied.

The boys rehearsed their handshake routine until they had it synchronized perfectly.

"I love it. Everyone's gonna be talkin' about our show. It's gonna be crazy!!!" Cameron jumped up and down with excitement.

"For sure. Ya, I like this. I just hope we don't mess up," Khalil said.

CHAPTER 8

The next morning, the boys met up with Cameron at the school basketball hoop. He was already decked out in a full Toronto Raptors throwback white pinstriped uniform with McGrady on the back. He dropped a large gym bag on the ground in front of Khalil, Dylan and Blake.

"Okay guys, take your pick. I brought extra jerseys, shorts, headbands, wristbands ... there's even a pair of basketball goggles somewhere in there."

The boys rummaged through the bag, removing colourful garments with different team names or cities written on them. Khalil saw a bright orange Syracuse jersey and immediately decided that it was for him. Dylan and Blake made their choices and began putting on the accessories to match the uniforms they took.

"Hey Blake, pass me those goggles right there," said

Cameron. He caught them and held them in front of Khalil.

"Airplane, you should wear these. They kinda look like aviator goggles. Y'know like what pilots wear. If you gonna be a pilot, you gotta dress the part, bro. It's perfect for you."

Khalil strapped the goggles around his head, trying to adjust them for a snug fit.

"Hey, he looks old school!" Blake said, pointing and laughing.

"Ya, like that Kareem Abdul guy we saw in the old school basketball highlights," said Dylan. "Looks cool."

"They feel funny," Khalil said. "You sure they don't look stupid?"

"They're perfect," said Cameron. "Remember it's a costume, so if it looks a lil' funny, who cares. Airplane, wear them. Trust me. You're the pilot. Y'know what ... you should find a scarf in the lost and found and wear that too. Jus' like a basketball fighter pilot."

Khalil shrugged his shoulders as Cameron continued. "Okay, so Blake, Dylan. This is the plan. Make sure you're wearing all this gear when you guys are sitting in the assembly. When they announce us and the music starts, you guys run from the audience to the stage and then we jus' party on stage. You know what I'm sayin'."

The boys high-fived each other with excitement and discussed what type of dunks they were going to do on stage before heading into homeroom.

Once in class, Ms. Kirkland prepped the students for the performance and let them know in what order they would go on stage. Cameron and Khalil were scheduled to go last and close out the show. This made Khalil even more nervous than he was before.

"Yo, Airplane. Don't even sweat it. We're gonna do great. Hey, let's see if Ms. Kirkland will let us go get that scarf from the lost and found."

Ms. Kirkland told the class they could do a final rehearsal while waiting to be called to the assembly. Cameron went to speak with her and quickly returned, showing two thumbs up.

"Let's go. See if we can find a white one. That's what I seen fighter pilots wearing on TV."

Cameron led Khalil to the front office where the lost and found bin was located. They both searched through it, pulling out sweaters, sneakers, and toys until Khalil found a puffy green scarf.

"Put that back. Keep looking, there's gotta be a white one in there," Cameron said. Khalil dove back into the box as Cameron's attention was diverted by Keri walking out of the office. She was in a different eighth-grade class.

"Whatchu doin' Cam, shopping for new used clothes?" Keri said, giggling.

"Funny. Nah, jus' trying to get our costume together for the assembly."

"Oh ya. Your class is performing. I'm so glad my teacher ain't making my class do that. I'd panic."

Khalil rose out of the bin victoriously, holding a cream-coloured scarf in hand. "I think we got one. Or at least this should be close enough," said Khalil before noticing Keri and suddenly becoming stiff and shy.

"Cam, who's your new friend?"

"Oh, ya. Keri, this is Airplane. Airplane meet Keri."

Khalil nervously shook Keri's tanned hand as Cameron continued, "Ya, he's new here. Used to live downtown Torono. We doing the performance together, so make sure you're there so you can see us."

Keri flipped her dirty blonde hair and smiled at Khalil, which made him melt instantly. "I sure will. I gotta get back to class. But I'll see you guys at the assembly. Airplane? Hmmm. I like that. Nice to meet you. Good luck."

Khalil was so timid that he could only nod his head and hypnotically wave his hand at Keri as she left.

"Dude ... I think she likes you," Cameron said.

Khalil just smiled bashfully.

* * *

Khalil stood backstage, rehearsing his lines repeatedly so he wouldn't forget any words once in front of the audience. The other students in the class were doing well with their performances. There was lots of applause and cheering for each act.

"Yo, Airplane. We're up next. You ready?"

Khalil nodded. He really wasn't ready, but he was already resigned to the fact that he had to go out on stage.

"Don't worry, bro. You gonna do great. We gonna shock the world!"

Ms. Kirkland patted the boys on the shoulders as she went onstage to introduce them.

"Alright now. You've been a great audience, and it's time for our final performance of the day. Please give a resounding applause for Khalil and Cam doing Basketball Rap!"

The audience clapped loudly, and the music began. Cameron and Khalil grabbed their props and rushed onto the stage. The audience cheered more loudly as they saw the boys giving each other fancy passes. Then the cheering grew even louder as they saw Blake and Dylan rushing the stage. Dylan held the basketball hoop while the others took turns dunking. Cameron jumped to the front of the stage and began his verse. Everybody jumped to their feet and danced as he rapped. They kept the noise going as Cameron flipped the ball to Khalil, who kept the rhythm going and the audience cheering. The energy in the gym increased as they continued. The boys were so hyped they even started dancing; doing whatever moves the music inspired them to do.

As the song was ending, Cameron ran out to the audience and grabbed students to go up on stage and dance with them. He even took Ms. Kirkland by the hand and led her out on stage. Soon the other students who had performed earlier joined, and the stage was packed with students yelling, "We love that basketball ... we love that basketball!"

The standing ovation lasted a of couple minutes, and Khalil couldn't believe that they were really clapping for him. Later that day, heading out to play basketball for lunch, the boys were mobbed by all the students in the hallway.

"You guys were amazing!"

"I never seen anything like that before."

"That was the best performance I've ever seen."

"You guys should be professionals and get record deals."

The boys slapped hands or got hugs from every student they passed. Being the most popular boy in school, Cameron was used to the attention. However, for Khalil, this was all very new. He had never been celebrated in this manner before. Except for maybe his birthday, but this feeling was like a birthday times one hundred. He was loving the praise. He was giddy but tried to follow Cameron's lead and act cool about it.

The mob followed them out to the basketball court and chanted, "We love that basketball ... we love that basketball!" as they began to play.

CHAPTER 9

Tryouts for the senior boys' basketball team were in full swing. After two weeks of intense drills and practice, the coach, Mr. Maracle, posted the team list outside the gym on the bulletin board. As soon as Khalil and Cameron got word that the final names had been posted, they darted to the gym at recess to see if they had made the team. Cameron already knew he had made it. He had been the team captain last year, so he knew he was almost guaranteed a spot on the team. Khalil, however, did not have the same confidence. He knew he had done his best, but prepared for the worst news.

"I don't think I'm gonna make the team," Khalil said as they headed to the gym. "I think I made too many mistakes last practice. Mr. Maracle didn't seem impressed with my play."

"Nah. You're good. Look, in such a short time, you've become one of the better players in the school. No one can jump as high as you or grab rebounds the way you do."

"Ya, but my shot is off. I keep missing too many open baskets."

"Don't worry. I know for sure you made it. And if you don't, then I will have to send a strongly worded email to Coach Maracle. Hahahaha."

Khalil couldn't laugh with Cameron. He was too anxious. A month ago, he couldn't care less about basketball. Now he didn't know what he would do if he got cut from the team. "I hope you're right, Cam. I really want to make the squad. I'm getting better every day. All the playing we've been doing has got to pay off, right?"

"Exactly! We got this bro. Jus' like the performance."

The boys started chanting the "We love that basketball" theme from the performance while doing their new handshake.

"Alright, now let's check this list," said Cameron.

A small group of boys huddled around the bulletin board outside the gym office. Some boys were high-fiving each other and celebrating with fist pumps as they saw their names on the list. While other boys walked away dejected, complaining under their breath after not seeing their names. Blake and Dylan came around the corner as Cameron found his name on the list.

"Hey Cam, you get cut?" Blake yelled jokingly.

Cameron turned around with his arms raised triumphantly. Pretending to celebrate as if he wasn't certain that his name would be there.

"Me? Get cut. Never. Not a chance, bro," Cameron yelled back. He pounded fists with a few of the other boys who saw their names posted as well. Meanwhile, Khalil scanned the list with his index finger. Dylan approached and leaned on Khalil's shoulder.

"Theeerrre's my name," said Dylan. "And look, there's yours, Airplane. I think. Your real name's Khalil, right?"

Khalil located his name and was overjoyed. This was going to be his first team. He had never played in an official league with uniforms and referees before. Any sport he played in the past was outside with a bunch of other kids. The ones clustered together would make up one team while the rest left standing would be the other. Nothing organized by adults.

Khalil slapped hands with Dylan and bumped his way through the crowd of boys still looking for their names.

"You guys made it, right?" Cameron said, holding both hands up.

"You know it," said Dylan as he and Khalil slapped him five at the same time.

"Nice! Yo, let's go out and play now. Hey Blake, c'mon, let's get outta here."

Khalil, Cameron and Dylan excitedly headed out to the basketball hoop. Khalil glanced back and noticed Blake still scanning the team list, but soon enough, Blake joined them. He followed slightly behind as the others talked enthusiastically about what the basketball season was going to be like and how well the team could do. Blake was quieter than usual, but Khalil was too excited to think much of it. Cameron turned to him. "Blake, what's wrong?"

"I ... I didn't make it," Blake whispered.

"What! No way. You sure? That's impossible." Cameron's face turned cherry-red.

"My name wasn't on the list." Blake's voice cracked as he spoke.

Catching wind of the conversation behind them, Dylan and Khalil slowed their pace and joined in.

"Must be a mistake," said Dylan. "Talk to Mr. Maracle about it."

"I dunno. Like I'm better than Peter and Joe. And for sure I know I'm better than Navdeep. Like c'mon now. Really! How is that little towel head making it before me!"

Khalil was shocked. Before he could fully register what he'd heard, Cameron replied, "Ya. That's true. That towel head ain't better than you. Do you see any towel heads in the NBA? Of course not! One-on-one, he can't beat you, so I dunno how he's making the team over you. Doesn't make sense. We should all speak with Mr. Maracle. Right, guys?"

Dylan and Blake were nodding in agreement.

Khalil looked at them with amazement. Once Dylan saw Khalil's eyes, he dropped his head, shame-faced.

"Right, Airplane?" Cameron repeated.

Khalil was so deep in his own thoughts that he didn't even hear his name called.

"Right Airplane ... yo, Airplane. You awake over there?"

"Huh. Oh ya. Right. Right," Khalil replied.

To Khalil, the bigger issue was how Blake and Cameron had referred to Navdeep. Much bigger than Blake not making the team. Khalil quickly realized he was the only one concerned about that, while the others were outraged about the team.

"We'll deal with this after school at practice. Don't sweat it, Blake. You're gonna be on the team. For now, let's just play," said Cameron.

CHAPTER 10

After school, the boys met at the gym for their first practice. Blake had decided he wouldn't bother going with the others. However, Cameron was adamant and pressured Dylan and Khalil to join him in speaking with the coach about Blake. They changed into their basketball gear and walked into the gym to the sound of bouncing balls and squeaking sneakers from the other boys, who were already shooting around.

In the equipment room, Mr. Maracle gathered pylons and basketballs for the practice.

"Hey Coach, how ya doin'?" said Cameron. "Do you mind if we have a word with you?"

Mr. Maracle, instantly alarmed by Cameron's tone, looked at the boys curiously.

"Certainly boys. Is there a problem? How can I assist?"

"Well, Coach, it's concerning our friend Blake. We feel ..."

Khalil tuned them out when he saw Navdeep chasing a loose ball rolling in their direction. Blake and Cameron's voices repeated the towel remark in Khalil's head as the ball rolled right up to his foot. A cyclone stirred in his belly as he stared at Navdeep. He didn't like what they had said about Navdeep. It suddenly clicked to Khalil; he couldn't advocate for Blake to be on the team. Not after that comment. Would it be fair to kick Navdeep off the team in favour of Blake who was so disrespectful? He bent over to retrieve the ball and tossed it to Navdeep. Navdeep waved "thank you" as Mr. Maracle began his response.

"Well, boys, I thank you for taking the time to address this with me. Blake is very lucky to have friends like you who would stand up for him. It's very difficult having to make cuts to the team. We only allow fifteen boys, so sometimes I have to make the difficult decision. I'm sorry boys, the decisions are final. To bring Blake on, we would have to cut someone else already granted a spot on the team, and that would not be fair to them. I hope you can understand. Once again, I'm very impressed with the three of you for speaking with me. I look forward to coaching you and having a stellar season. I have a good feeling about you guys."

His face turning crimson, Cameron was visibly upset; Dylan too, but not nearly as much, while Khalil fought to keep the corner of his lips from curling into a smile. He felt justified by Mr. Maracle's response and was relieved he didn't have to tell the other boys that he didn't believe Blake deserved their backing. The boys joined the rest of the team, putting up shots but not saying anything to each other. Khalil took a deep shot from the three-point line and missed. The rebound bounced towards Cameron but his attention was elsewhere. The ball rolled to the corner while Khalil noticed Cameron shaking his head in disappointment, staring at Navdeep. Blake's comment echoed in Khalil's mind again, and then Cameron's voice followed, booming and intolerant. Khalil thought his mind was playing tricks on him. He tried to ignore it. Cameron wasn't the one who made the initial comment, so Khalil wondered if Cameron was really that intolerant or if Cameron was just upset that his good friend wasn't going to be on the team.

TWEEET!! Coach Maracle blew the whistle and instructed the team to sit at centre court. "Hello, boys. I'm glad to see all of you. Congratulations first of all for making the roster. You should be proud of yourselves. There was a lot of competition this year. A lot of good players in this school and you were chosen to be here because of the skills you've displayed. Well done. All of you."

Khalil listened carefully as Mr. Maracle conveyed his expectations for the team. This was his first coach, and Khalil wanted to impress him enough to possibly get a starting position on the team. He looked around the gym at the other players. He knew that Cameron and Dylan would likely be starters. Then there was Shawn; he was the tallest on the team. Everyone called him Stretch because he was six-foot-four, head and shoulders above everyone else. He was a good shooter, but he moved slowly. There were times Khalil had outjumped and outhustled him for rebounds out on the playground. Khalil figured Stretch would start too and measured himself against Stretch's abilities.

Khalil felt good about his chances of getting one of the other two starting positions. As he continued to survey the room, his eyes landed on Navdeep. He chuckled to himself at the realization that he and Navdeep were the only dark-skinned players on the team. Them and Mr. Maracle, who was of the First Nation Ojibwa people. If Navdeep wasn't on the team, Khalil would really feel like a minority. At least now, he and Navdeep had that in common; that gave Khalil some comfort. Prior to attending this school, Khalil didn't think very much about race. Most of the kids in his old neighbourhood looked like him. The school he attended was mixed with kids of all nationalities, and they all got along.

"So I hope you are prepared to sweat today. We've got a lot of practice to do in very little time. Our first game will be next weekend. We'll be playing in the Cooksville exhibition tournament at the Natural Springs Sportsplex. Not too far from here in Mississauga. Your parents will have to drop you off Saturday morning, and we'll be taking a team bus from the school."

The boys yelped with excitement and began talking amongst each other.

"Coach, what teams will we be playing against at the tourney?" Cameron asked.

"I know there'll be a few Mississauga and Brampton schools. Oakville too. Mainly teams that are not in our division. Teams that we probably won't play again unless we make it to Regionals. But it will be a good chance to see how we measure up to some of the best teams in the West End."

Mr. Maracle motioned for the boys to stand.

"Alright, let's get to work. Layup drill. Gimme two lines, one for rebounding and the other for layups. Nothing lazy, let's move at game speed. Let's go!"

The boys jumped to their feet and followed Mr. Maracle's instructions. After layups, they ran jump shot drills. Next, they did two-on-one fast breaks, then three-on-two fast breaks, rebounding drills and lots of running. Mr. Maracle wanted this team to be in top condition so they could outrun any team they played against. They finished with a quick scrimmage.

As the boys were taking their water break, Mr. Maracle spread out the team uniforms on the court. They were gold with navy blue trim, in line with the school colours and mascot, which was a jaguar. Each jersey had a headshot of a ferocious-looking jaguar on the chest and the school name C. Alexander Sr. PS written in navy blue below. Pen and clipboard in hand, Mr. Maracle called out to the players. "Okay boys, everyone come and choose a uni. The ones on the left are large, these here in the middle are medium size and on the right are the smalls. Choose your fit and let me know what number you have so I can record it here on our team list."

The boys snatched at jerseys, trying to get their favourite number before anyone else could grab it. Khalil took his time. He didn't have a favourite number and wasn't sure which one he wanted to take. Through the commotion, there was one number no one was reaching for; number thirteen. Khalil scooped up the jersey and put it on over his T-shirt. It was a perfect fit.

"Ohhh. Lucky number thirteen, eh?" said Dylan sarcastically.

The other boys in the gym looked at Khalil in the number thirteen jersey and recoiled. They were superstitious and thought that wearing thirteen would be bad luck, but Khalil didn't feel that way. He smiled and popped the collar of the jersey with both hands in a flaunting manner. This was his first uniform. Feeling fresh, Khalil thought nothing could stop him from being the high-level basketball player he was dreaming about becoming.

CHAPTER 11

Saturday morning Khalil hugged his mother in the car as she reminded him what numbers to call in case of emergency.

"Don't worry, Mom. Everything's going to be okay. I'm not going to get hurt. It's just basketball. I've been playing every day for the last couple months and look, I'm fine."

"Still, you need to be careful, understand? As a nurse, I see kids come into the hospital all the time with twisted, sprained or broken ankles from playing sports. Mainly basketball. So don't tell me not to worry. You just need to be careful! Okay?"

"Yes, Mommy. I promise. I'll be careful." Khalil opened the car door and waved bye to his mother. Being careful was the last thing on his mind. He was too excited to play his first league game in his brand-new uniform.

"You have your lunch, right, honey?"

"Yes, Mom, I have it!" Khalil replied, slightly irritated.

"Alright. Have fun. I'll be back to pick you up this evening."

Khalil felt that his mother couldn't leave fast enough. He ran to join the rest of the team, waiting for the bus in front of the school.

"AIRPLANE!!!!" the boys shouted as he hustled over. He and Cameron did their signature handshake, and then Khalil dapped fists with all the boys, including Mr. Maracle, who was taking attendance.

"Okay, that's everybody. We should be good to go as soon as the bus arrives," he said.

A few minutes later, the school bus creaked from around the corner and screeched to a halt in front of the boys. Mr. Maracle greeted the driver and confirmed their destination before advising the boys to enter and find a seat. Each boy rushed in and took a double seat for themselves and their gym bags. Khalil took a seat near the middle of the bus and sat close to the window. Cameron was in the seat behind and leaned over the green vinyl, white-trimmed back of Khalil's seat to talk with him.

"Bro. This is gonna be great. I promise you. Tournaments are the most fun. You said this is your first time, right?"

"Yup," Khalil said while nodding.

"Don't worry about a thing. When we get there, we find what courts we're playing on, scout some of the teams we might play against and then game time!"

"I just hope I play good. Hope we all do," Khalil said.

"I jus' hope we win," Dylan said from the seat across from Khalil.

"Me too," yelled Cameron, which seemed to inspire the

rest of the bus to reply one after the other.

"Ya, me too."

"Me three."

"Me four."

"Ya, we better win. Gotta rep for our school."

"Gotta rep for the Jaguars!"

In unison, some of the boys started growling while others chanted, "Go Jaguars! Urrrrrrr. Go Jaguars!"

The boys laughed and joked with each other until the bus came to a stop in front of the Natural Springs Centre. The boys filed out of the bus staring at the giant sportsplex, which they were about to enter. Khalil was amazed; he had seen the building many times from the highway when driving with his parents and had always wondered what the inside looked like. It was a massive building. The boys walked in and immediately looked up at the ceiling, which seemed to be higher than the clouds were outside. The lobby was bright, spacious, and busy with people. Mr. Maracle led the boys to the sportsplex map and directory. Straight ahead were three indoor dome soccer fields, the gymnastics gym and fitness centres. To the right were six ice rinks and racquetball courts, a martial arts studio and fencing space. There was a baseball and softball training centre and a rock climbing gym to the left. Mr. Maracle located the basketball courts on the floor below.

"Alright boys, looks like we're downstairs. Follow me."

The boys walked behind their coach looking left, looking right, up and down as if they were tourists in a foreign city. Once downstairs, they saw other boys in colourful uniforms walking and congregating in the hallway. Above their heads were signs that indicated the entrance to each court. There were five of them. Mr. Maracle scanned his clipboard for confirmation. "Okay, says here that we're on Court Three to start. Let's check it out."

As they walked in, Cameron nudged Khalil on the arm. "Look at that guy there. He looks like a grown man. He can't be our age."

Khalil turned his attention to a six-foot-seven massive-looking man with a boy's face. His dark complexion and sweat further revealed his muscular frame. He was twice the size of Mr. Maracle. All the boys stared at him with dread in their eyes.

"We don't have to play against him, do we?" said Dylan.

"Hope not," said Stretch.

"You gonna have to guard him, Stretch, if we do," said Cameron.

"You guys gonna have to help me. Like triple-team him or something."

"Maybe he's not a good player. Maybe he's just big. Never know," said Khalil.

All the boys looked at Khalil as if he was crazy and started laughing.

"Oh, he can play. Jus' lookit him. There's no doubt he can ball. And every team is in trouble when he does," Cameron said.

The boys walked out onto Court Three. They followed Mr. Maracle to a bench that had a sign with their school name on it.

"This is our side, boys. Drop your stuff and go warm up.

Cam, you lead warm-ups. Start with a couple laps, then get into layup lines. Our game starts in ten minutes," said Mr. Maracle while pointing at the score clock displaying time winding down.

The boys quickly headed out to the court to begin their warm-up while Mr. Maracle went to speak with the referees and score-keepers. The other team entered while the Jaguars were running laps. They watched them through the corner of their eyes, sizing up the other team, still trying to follow Cameron's lead. The other team was dressed in white uniforms with red and black trim and the face of a mean-looking bulldog on the leg of their shorts. They were from St. Peter's Catholic, a school in Mississauga. Khalil recognized the name and mascot from the uniform that his cousin Renee wore to school. She was a star basketball player and always bragged about how good her school was in sports, so Khalil began to get nervous. With two minutes on the clock, Mr. Maracle gathered the team by the bench.

"Okay, boys. It all begins now. It's alright to be nervous. That's a natural feeling. It means you're alive, and the adrenaline is ready to flow. Turn your nervousness into excitement and have fun out there. Do what we've practiced, play hard, and you will be rewarded. I promise you that. I can't promise that we'll win, but if we play the right way, we'll give ourselves a chance. Okay, so Cameron and Dylan, you guys start at guards. In the frontcourt, Stretch, you play centre. Kelly, you start at small forward. And starting at power forward will be Khalil."

Thrilled to hear his name called in the starting line-up, Khalil unconsciously made a small fist pump that only

Cameron noticed and nudged Khalil to congratulate him.

"Remember to stay disciplined on defence and don't give up anything easy to these guys. Make them work for everything. Okay. Hands in." Mr. Maracle punched his fist into the middle of the huddle. The boys did the same.

"Jags on three. ONE, TWO, THREE!"

"JAGS!!!" the boys yelled and sprinted to mid-court, where the Bulldogs were already waiting for them. The Jaguar players bumped fists with the Bulldogs while getting into position for the jump ball. The referees approached and wished both teams luck while advising them about fair play and sportsmanship. The boys nodded their understanding and braced for the jump as if they were frozen in place posing for a picture.

The referee held the ball between Stretch and the Bulldog's centre, then blew the whistle and tossed it high between the two boys. True to his name, Stretch stretched his long arm as high as he could and tipped the ball forward. The ball sailed towards Khalil's side of the jump circle. With hunger in his eyes, Khalil chased after the ball, securing it for his team before any of the opposing players could touch it. Now that Khalil had the ball, he looked around at all the players. His mind went blank, not knowing what he should do next.

CHAPTER 12

"Go!" Mr. Maracle yelled towards Khalil, which snapped him out of his panic. Khalil suddenly realized no one was between him and the Bulldogs' basket, so he dribbled awkwardly towards it. His ball control wasn't smooth. The ball ricocheted off his knees a couple of times, but he managed to keep it from bouncing too far away from his body. Defenders chased him as he scooped the ball up and leaped toward the basket. Two of the Bulldog players rammed into Khalil as he laid the ball off the backboard and into the basket. Khalil crashed to the floor with the two Bulldog defenders on top of him.

"TWEET!!" went the referee's whistle. "And one! Basket's good," the referee yelled. The Jaguar players ran over to Khalil, screaming enthusiastically. Cameron, Stretch, Dylan and Kelly together pulled Khalil off the ground and celebrated. Disoriented at first, Khalil tried to understand what had happened, but when he saw his teammate's reaction, he realized he had made the basket.

The Jaguar players on the bench were yelling, jumping and punching the air. Khalil saw their celebration and was immediately filled with confidence. The referees blew their whistles, trying to calm the boys down and get them into position for the free throw. Khalil stepped to the line and focused on the orange ring in front of him. Khalil knew he wasn't the best shooter, but he had practiced free throws as often as he could. He had a routine that seemed to help him shoot better. He closed his eyes, whispered, "Thank you" while imagining the ball going into the rim, then opened his eyes and took the shot. The ball plunged through the net and the Jaguars continued their celebration.

That play set the tone for the remainder of the game. The Jaguars led the whole way and won convincingly forty-eight to thirty-two. Khalil and Cameron led the team in scoring. Khalil with seventeen points and twelve rebounds. Cameron finished with twenty points and seven assists. After the game, Mr. Maracle led the boys up to the balcony bleachers; to get there, they had to leave through the same door they entered and go up the stairs at the end of the hallway. The bleachers were wide enough that they overlooked all five basketball courts. They set up camp between Court One and Court Two to watch the game that was about to start and scout the competition.

"Hey guys, eat your snacks, your fruit or power bars now so you have enough energy for the next game. Down there is another school from the Halton Region that we may have to play during the regular season, so get a good look at them and their tendencies. It will give us an edge when we play them. We played the first game very well. I'd like to see us carry that momentum forward."

"Thanks, Coach!" Cameron said while chewing on a green apple. "You think we're good enough to beat them?"

"I think we're good enough to win this tournament, but anything could happen. You have to respect your opponent's ability to capitalize on your weaknesses. Once you recognize that, you can guard against their game plan. Okay, look, the game's about to start."

Most of the boys got up and stood at the bottom bleacher leaning against the pole railing, meant to prevent anyone from falling off the balcony. The schools playing were John Roberts S.P. from Oakville and Chris Hadfield from Milton. From the jump, the boys could see that the Chris Hadfield team was much stronger. Every player could shoot from a long distance and they were quick defensively; didn't give up easy baskets. While most of the team was paying attention to that game, Cameron's attention was on Court Two.

"Yo, Dylan. Airplane. Look over here. That big guy's team is about to play," said Cameron.

The boys hung their arms over the railing while watching the man-child in awe. In the layup line, they watched him glide above the rim and gently drop the ball into the hoop.

"Wow!" said Dylan. "He could prolly jus' dunk that with his elbows if he wanted. He's bigger than my father. I can't believe this guy."

"I can't believe this whole team. They all are big. And that guy has a moustache," said Cameron.

"Ya. And that one over there has a beard. They look like a high school team. What school is that?" said Khalil.

The boys squinted to get a closer look at the team jerseys. They wore black uniforms with gold trim and a picture of a panther jumping through the letter D on their shorts.

"I think that says Darcel Sr. Public across their chests," Cameron said in a shaky voice.

"Isn't that in ...?" Dylan began wide-eyed.

"Malton!" Cameron and Dylan said simultaneously with a fearful look on their faces.

Khalil was confused by the look they gave. Saying the name Malton alone seemed to strike their spirit with terror.

"No wonder they look like ... like ..." Cameron searched for a description, holding his hands on his cheeks. "... like Team Nigeria."

Khalil looked at his friends skeptically, but he couldn't help but notice that the Darcel team was the exact opposite of his team. While Khalil and Navdeep were the only dark-skinned players for their squad, Darcel was all dark-skinned kids; African, Caribbean and East Indian, except for two boys.

"Noooo wooonnder," Dylan replied. "I hope we don't have to play those guys. They'll slaughter us."

Khalil watched Cameron nodding his head in agreement. For the remainder of the game, Khalil listened to stories about times driving through Malton that scared them, or tales about menacing Malton kids they heard from older siblings. Other teammates who heard also joined in with their own fables about how dangerous Malton was and how they would never go there after dark. All except for

Navdeep, who had enough of their stories. "I used to live in Malton. It's not like you guys say. It's not bad. It's just regular people. Those are regular kids down there. Bigger than us ... okay sure. But they regular just like us."

Navdeep bumped Khalil's shoulder with his elbow and made a face as if to say, "Can you believe these guys!" To Khalil all the talk sounded like blah blah blah. He heard stories about Malton too, but never took them seriously enough to be afraid of the place or the kids from there. Khalil was from Toronto, so from his perspective, whatever people were saying was going on in Malton was happening in Toronto too, so he had no worries.

The Darcel team destroyed their opponent fifty-six to seventeen, which further punctuated the fear and folklore swirling through the minds of Khalil's teammates. They were chattering about the game when Mr. Maracle called out for the team to get ready.

"We're next guys. Our game is on Court One. They just finished up, so let's head down and warm up."

The boys hurried down, passing other teams on their way to Court One. The Darcel team was filtering into the hallway, celebrating as the Jaguars were walking by. They stared open-mouthed at the Darcel kids, who didn't seem to even notice the Jaguar players. Khalil stared too, but not with the same astonishment as his teammates. The manchild noticed Khalil's glare and nodded his chin upwards as if to say, "What's up? Whatchu lookin' at?" Khalil returned the nod and headed into the gym.

"Do you know that guy? Did he say anything to you?" asked Kelly animatedly.

Annoyed by the question, Khalil shook his head and kept walking to their bench. The team they were set to play was the Oakville Middle School Spartans. Red uniforms with black and white trim. Despite being a speedy team, the Spartans weren't very tall and didn't play much defence which the Jaguars quickly took advantage of. Stretch dominated in the paint, scoring fifteen points and grabbing fifteen rebounds. Cameron scored ten points but dished out ten assists. However, Khalil led the team, scoring eighteen points and pulling down twenty-one rebounds; the way he and Stretch hit the offensive boards, the Spartans didn't have a chance.

The win qualified the Jaguars for the semi-finals, coincidentally against the other Milton team, the Chris Hadfield Hawks. They were scheduled to play on Court Three again. After their warm-up, Mr. Maracle gave a quick pep talk.

"Boys, a win here will put us in the finals. We watched this team earlier; we know their strength is their shooting. We cannot give them any open shots. Our defence must be solid. Contest everything. Number Seven is probably their best player. He can shoot from anywhere on the court. Khalil, it will be your job to slow him down."

Khalil nodded at Mr. Maracle as he continued. "It's got to be a group effort. Help each other and talk on defence so we know where they are and where they're going at all times."

As the starters walked to centre court for the jump ball, Cameron huddled them together quickly. "Hey listen. Let's run these guys out of the gym. We're the best team from Milton here and we're gonna show them. Suffocating defence. Let's lock them down. Alright? Alright!"

The boys responded, "For sure, yah, no doubt. Let's get 'em!"

They all got into position for the tip and the referee threw the ball high in the air.

CHAPTER 13

The Hawks won the tip and raced towards the Jaguars' basket. The Jaguars recovered quickly, preventing an easy score. They forced the Hawks to kick the ball back out to the three-point line where Number Seven was poised to put up from long range. As he caught the ball, Number Seven rose to throw up his shot. He was focused and knew he was about to drain the three, but before he could raise the ball above his head, Khalil slapped down on the ball, knocking it out of his hands. Khalil quickly scooped up the ball and threw it the length of the court where Cameron was sprinting towards the Hawks' basket. Cameron caught the lob pass in stride and finished with an uncontested layup.

The defensive play and score energized the Jaguars. When Cameron ran back down the court, he slapped hands with Khalil hard enough that it could be heard above all the cheering and yelling. They glared at each other as if to say, "We can't be stopped!" then picked up their man on the defensive.

The Hawks knew immediately they were in for a fight. They didn't back down. Number Seven and Number Eleven for the Hawks put up three-point shots whenever they were in range. No dribbling, just catch and shoot. They knew if they tried to put the ball on the floor, the Jaguars would steal it immediately. At the end of the half, the Jaguars held a five-point lead, thirty-two to twenty-seven. It was a high-scoring game despite both teams playing strong defensively. The difference in the game was the Jaguars offensive rebounding and the Hawks three-point shooting.

"NO MORE THREES!" howled Mr. Maracle. "You guys have to deny the pass. Don't even let Seven or Eleven catch the ball out there. Force them to dribble. Once we get them in the paint, we can trap them. They have nowhere to go other than into Stretch's big mittens. But be aware of the kick-out for three. We shut that down, then they can't keep up with us, alright?"

The boys nodded, their eyes fixed on the words flying out of Mr. Maracle's mouth.

"Get out there and let's take control of this game. Khalil and Jessie, you are our best defenders. Cover Seven and Eleven. Stick to them. No more points. We'll live with the other players scoring, but not them. Got it!"

"Got it, Coach!" the boys bawled and hustled back onto the court.

The game resumed, and it was a back-and-forth battle. Although Khalil and Jessie were able to limit the Hawks' Number Seven and Number Eleven's production, the other Hawks players picked up the slack and kept the score close. They were all decent shooters. As the game wound down to the one-minute mark, Cameron used a screen from Stretch to get by his defender and skated to the basket for a layup giving the Jaguars a three-point lead with a score of fifty-four to fifty-one. The Hawks' coach eagerly called a timeout. His eyes were on fire. Upset that his team's defence allowed Cameron to break through. Mr. Maracle addressed the Jaguars, who were bent over, dripping with sweat, holding the bottom of their shorts.

"Stand up straight, boys. Don't let them see how tired you are. Don't think about being tired. Think about winning this game. We play solid defence for the next minute and that's it. Then you can lie down if you want. But while the clock is running, we stand strong. Jessie, you come in for Navdeep and cover Number Eleven. I believe Number Fifteen will inbound the ball. Kelly, that's your man. I want you to sag off him and help Jessie double team Number Eleven so he doesn't catch the inbound pass. Khalil, you already know not to let Number Seven catch the pass, either. Let's get a steal here and the game is over. Hands in!"

The boys layered their hands over Mr. Maracle's fist in the middle of the huddle.

Mr. Maracle hollered, "ONE TWO THREE!!"

The boys roared, "JAGUARS!!!"

Just as Mr. Maracle predicted, the Hawks' Number Fifteen stood out of bounds to toss the ball in. The Jaguars took their places, sticking close to the player they were defending. As the referee handed the ball to Number Fifteen, he was surprised to see no one guarding him and the ball. The referee silently began the five-second count, showing each number with his fingers. The Hawks' players desperately tried to break free from the Jaguars' defence, but no one could get open. Number Fifteen was alarmed when he saw the referee throw up four fingers. Kelly had his back to Number Fifteen as he double-teamed Number Eleven. So, Number Fifteen tossed the ball off Kelly's backside, jumped inbounds, then scooped the ball up and began dribbling towards the Jaguars' basket.

Realizing what happened, the Jaguars scrambled to stop the ball, leaving Hawks' players who were once covered now wide open. Stretch and Khalil jumped in front of Number Fifteen to prevent him from scoring. Number Fifteen quickly adjusted and looked out to the three-point line for a teammate to pass to. Both Number Seven and Number Eleven were open. He flung the ball in their direction. Reading his mind, Khalil reached out and tipped the pass. The ball ricocheted off players on both teams until it landed back in the hands of the Hawks' Number Fifteen, who pulled up from three and drained the shot to tie the game. Mr. Maracle immediately called a timeout with twenty seconds left in the game.

"Okay, boys, shake it off. Tough break. They got a little lucky that time. But good defence. Make sure you never have your back to the player inbounding the ball. Always see the ball. Listen, we have the last shot. Let's win the game with it."

Mr. Maracle drew up the end of game-play and sent the boys onto the court. Khalil inbounded to Stretch. Since he was the tallest one on the court, there would be less of a chance the Hawks could steal the inbound pass. Stretch handed the ball off to Cameron, who dribbled to his favourite spot on the floor: left corner of the free-throw line. He dribbled behind his back, then crossed over in front to lose the defender and put up the shot with five seconds on the clock. Cameron held his follow-through stance on his toes, shooting hand still high in the air, fingers pointed at the rim. He knew the ball was going in. While everyone in the gym looked like statues watching the ball float towards the basket, Khalil was boxing out Hawks' players in case the ball bounced off the rim. And that's exactly what it did.

The ball hit the right side of the rim where Khalil had claimed real estate. He jumped as soon as the ball hit and tipped it back above the cylinder before the buzzer went off. As the ball trickled into the net, Khalil ran towards centre court with both fists high above his head. He was mobbed by his teammates, who ran at him from all directions and piled on top of him in celebration.

CHAPTER 14

After the win, Mr. Maracle led the Jaguars back up to the bleachers to watch the rest of the other semi-final game featuring the Darcel Panthers and another Mississauga team, the Clarkson Middle School Warriors. There were still five minutes left in the game, but the game was already over. The Panthers led by thirty points and the Warriors looked like they didn't want to play any longer.

"Whoa. The Warriors are getting run out of the gym. They got no chance now," said Cameron.

"Ya dude. Darcel is unbeatable," said Dylan.

"We can't beat them. Look at them!" Stretch said.

Other players joined in, expressing how difficult it will be to play against the Panthers. Mr. Maracle overheard them speaking.

"Listen, boys. That team is good. It's very evident. But

so are we. Don't count yourselves out before we even play. Believe in yourselves. Don't psych yourselves out. Every team has a weakness that can be exploited. We have to find their weakness and build on our strengths. If we focus on that, then anything ... anything can happen. But you have to have faith."

The boys listened quietly; most weren't buying what Mr. Maracle was selling. They didn't believe they had a chance against the Panthers. Khalil let Mr. Maracle's words penetrate and decided he was not going to be scared. He decided he was going to do everything in his power to get a win for the Jaguars. Khalil felt a jolt of energy and excitement ignite in his chest. His eyes flashed with intensity. He was ready to beat the Panthers. His face was brilliant with focus. Khalil peered over at Cameron, whose face was also beaming. They nodded at each other, acknowledging that they weren't going to be intimidated by any other team, no matter what the odds were.

The boys tried to relax before their championship game while watching the consolation final. Most of the players were restless. Some paced back and forth through the bleachers while others sat trying to suppress jittery legs. Cameron and Khalil were the opposite. They discussed game strategy; how to use the pick-and-roll offense to create an advantage against the Panthers.

"Okay, let's head down. It's almost time," said Mr. Maracle. "Same as usual, warm up at game speed. Break a sweat. This is the championship. We have to be ready when the whistle blows. C'mon, let's go. We're on Court Three."

The team followed Mr. Maracle down to the court.

They were as silent as a funeral procession. They held their heads down as they passed the Panthers, who were already on the court shooting around. Some of the Panther players smirked when they saw the Jaguars, knowing instantly that they had an edge over the other team. They could smell the fear. The buzzer sounded, and the Jaguars left the huddle after Mr. Maracle's pre-game speech. Khalil shook his head in disappointment when their usual enthusiastic pre-game chant of "one, two, three—JAGS" sounded dispirited and droopy.

"C'mon guys. Look alive. We got this. We can do this. Leave it all on the floor. If we do our best, we can't ask for anything else. Good things will happen!" said Khalil as the starters headed to centre court for the jump ball. They nodded a little more confidently until they were standing face to face with the Panthers for the tip. Panic returned when they pounded fists with the Panthers, who towered over them before the referee held the ball between Stretch and the Panthers' big man. He chuckled confidently when he saw Stretch's hands trembling. The referee tossed the ball up, and they both jumped for it. Except it didn't look like Stretch jumped because the Panthers' big man skied well above Stretch's head, tipping the ball forward to one of his teammates racing to the basket. He scored before any of the Jaguars could even react.

The Jaguars inbounded the ball, Cameron dribbled to the top of the key on the Panthers' end. He threw a pass to Kelly on the wing, who then dumped the ball down to Stretch in the paint. Stretch tried to back down the Panthers' big man. He faked left, then tried a turnaround jump shot, but the Panthers' big man immediately swatted it back into his hands. Stretch tried another move and put up another shot, but that was clapped out of his grasp and down the court where a Panthers' guard snaffled it up on a fast break and scored. Most of the possessions to begin the game went this way, with the Panthers either blocking a shot or stealing the ball for fast break points. The Panther lead was twelve to zero when Mr. Maracle called his first timeout.

"Hey! Wake up out there. You look like you're walking in mud. Put some life in your legs. Let's not make it easier for them. They don't need our help. Protect the ball and set each other up to score!"

Cameron and Khalil pounded fists as they left the huddle. They knew if they were going to have any chance of coming back in the game, it would be through their hands. In their first play out of the timeout, Khalil set a pick on Cameron's defender getting him open just long enough for him to hit a jumper from his favourite spot.

The Panthers responded by lobbing the ball up to their big man, who dominantly reached above Stretch's hand and dropped the ball into the hoop. He did it so easily that it looked like he was playing against a toddler. Back down the court, Khalil and Cameron worked the pick-and-roll again, this time when the defence jumped out at Cameron he dropped a bounce pass to Khalil who rolled down the lane and shot a high floater just above the outstretched hands of the Panthers' big man for the score. The teams traded baskets for a while, but by halftime, the Panthers' lead had ballooned to twenty points with a score of thirty-eight to eighteen.

Mr. Maracle gave his halftime speech and the boys sat silently, distraught, waiting to hear the buzzer to alert them that the second half was set to begin. Cameron leaned over to Khalil and whispered, "Airplane, it's jus' you and me. Everyone else is too scared. We gotta do everything. So let's do it!"

"Yah man. Let's do it. Two-man game," Khalil said.

The boys ran out onto the court for the second half. Cameron and Khalil raised the intensity as soon as the ball was inbounded. They clamped down on defence. They got steals and forced difficult shots. Cameron pestered the Panthers' guards, making them dribble the ball off their own legs. Khalil switched with Stretch to guard the Panthers' big man and was able to slow him down. There was no stopping him, but Khalil's effort and lack of fear prevented him from dominating. The Jaguars were cutting into the lead. The Panthers' big man became uneasy now that Khalil was defending him. So much so that he threw up an air ball which Khalil caught and hurled up the court toward Cameron in one motion. He landed on the ground and slid into the padding against the wall.

Cameron dove for the ball at the same time as the Panthers' point guard. They collided and the struggle to secure the ball quickly became a wrestling match with the two pulling and swinging at each other. Khalil heard the commotion before he saw it and ran over at top speed. By the time he got to the scuffle, the two were on their feet and Panthers had surrounded Cameron. They all looked like they were ready to pounce on him. Khalil heard the Panthers' point guard yelling at Cameron, "Guh 'head snowflake, say it. Say it! I dare you, racist. Finish what you were sayin'. I'll knock you out, bruh!"

Cameron nervously scanned the faces of the Panthers' players, each with fists clenched, anxious to hear his next words. Cameron didn't dare utter another word. Just stood there until Khalil and Dylan jumped in between. The referees quickly ran in to separate the boys before fists could fly. They issued technical fouls, then ejected Cameron and the Panthers' point guard from the remainder of the game.

After the incident, the Jaguars were completely deflated. They couldn't do anything right. Khalil tried his best to keep them in the game, but it quickly got out of hand, with the Panthers taking a lead of more than thirty points. The game finished with the Panthers winning seventy-six to forty-three. It was an embarrassing loss for the Jaguars. The only bright spot was Khalil's thirty points and twenty-two rebounds. Impressed with Khalil, the Panthers pounded fists with him, acknowledging his effort and showing respect.

"Yeow, you played good, fam. Don't see many who got heart like you," said the Panthers' big man. "You should come out to our hood. We get good runs. Mans dem come from all over the city. Better competition … but yeow, 'sup wit you mans over there. Was about to say sumpin' you can't take back. Feel me? I know he your boy and all, but you better watch out for him. Choose your friends wisely."

Khalil gave a confused look while shaking hands with the Panthers' big man. Then headed straight for Cameron on the bench. They pounded fists and gathered their belongings.

"Tough game," said Khalil.

"Tell me about it. I swear we could've came back. I'm so mad. That ... guy got me kicked out the game."

"So Cam. What happened out there? How did the fight start? What does he think you said to him?"

Cameron looked away from Khalil uneasily. "Nuttin', man. It wasn't nuttin'. I dunno what his problem was."

CHAPTER 15

The Monday morning at school, the boys met at the basketball court as usual. Players from the team, along with others, were playing American Twenty-One. As Khalil approached, he saw Keri with her friends, talking with Dylan and Cameron.

"There he is!" yelled Dylan. "Superstar."

Khalil jokingly turned around to see if they were talking about someone else behind him.

"Hi Airplane," Keri said. Her girlfriends repeated the greeting in chorus, making Khalil blush.

"The guys were just saying how good you played at the tournament. You guys made it to the championship. That's amazing!"

"Ya, but we lost pretty badly."

"But you played good, though, right?" Keri said, leaning

her shoulder onto Khalil's arm. Caught off guard by the contact, Khalil stiffened up as if he had done something wrong. Keri and her girlfriends giggled at his reaction.

"Oh, Airplane was good. Better than good," Cameron cut in. "I can't help but feel somewhat responsible since I taught him how to play. Hahahahaha."

Blake approached the group and began dapping fists with the boys. Keri held out her fist with a look on her face that said, "What about me?" Blake shrugged his shoulders and dapped the girls too. They all laughed.

"So you guys win on the weekend or what?" Blake said.

"They lost in the championship," Keri blurted out before Cameron could answer.

"Who's telling this story? Like were you even there?" Cameron said.

"Sheeeesh saaaaarraaay," Keri said.

"Thank you!" said Cameron as some of the boys playing diverted their attention to Cameron telling the story. "Now, we lost in the championship."

"I said that part already," Keri teased.

Cameron playfully looked at Keri side-eyed and continued, "Like I said, we made it to the championship, but we had to play against this super team. Like, they all looked like high school students."

"Some of them had beards!" Dylan chimed in.

"Ya, they were big guys. It was unfair from the start. They didn't even have no white guys on the team. Okay, wait, maybe one. But the rest were like ... they were like Team Nigeria," Cameron stated.

The group of kids all gasped, looking at each other with

wonder. Khalil shuddered to hear Cameron's description of the team but didn't say anything.

"They were from Malton!" Dylan joined in.

The group of kids gasped again, this time louder. Some gulped heavily.

"Whoa!" a few of the listeners wailed.

"Ya, Malton kids. So you know what that means," Cameron said to the group of fearful faces, anxious to hear his next words. "They had this one big, big Black guy. No one could stop him. He was a grown man playing with boys. He had muscles everywhere, even his fingers looked ripped. I still don't think he could be our age. No way. He looked like he was twenty-one ..."

Khalil tuned out Cameron's story as he was feeling uncomfortable hearing it. He persuaded himself that Cameron hadn't said anything really wrong, but something about the story and the reaction from the other kids didn't sit well with him. Khalil was thinking that if he were telling the story, he wouldn't have mentioned that the team was Black or that they were from Malton. To Khalil, those were not important details, but apparently to everyone else, that was the story.

"Airplane? Is that right? Hello, Airplane, are you in there?" Keri said, snapping Khalil out of his thoughts.

"Huh?" said Khalil

"Is it true? That guy stepped to you?"

"What? Oh, you mean after the game? That ummm ... big Black guy?" Khalil winced as he heard himself use the same description he was uncomfortable hearing the other kids use. "Ya, it was nothing. He was just saying wassup.

Said I should come play at their park. That's all."

"What? You're not gonna go, are you?" said Keri.

"I wouldn't go out there if I were you," Blake joined in.

Khalil heard a chorus of "yahs" and "don't do it's" from the group. Khalil asked himself why he called the Panthers' big man, the big Black guy. It's not what he intended to say. It just came out. He looked at Keri, who was staring at him wide-eyed, waiting for him to continue. She looked so pretty Khalil wanted to keep her attention on him.

"Maybe I won't go out there. That guy was scary. That Black guy was ... he was a beast." Khalil cringed as he heard himself again, but kept talking because Keri was hanging on his every word. The school buzzer sounded, rescuing Khalil from further compromising himself.

In class, Khalil half-listened to the morning announcements over the PA system. He was replaying the conversation with Keri in his mind. Cursing himself for making the big Black guy comments. He knew if it were a big white guy, no one would describe him that way. They would just call him big. His colour wouldn't be part of the description.

"And next we want to congratulate the senior boys' basketball team. Our Jaguars finished second in their tournament this weekend. A special shout-out goes to our very own Khalil Harris aka The Airplane! He won MVP honours for the team. We're very proud of him. So make sure when you see him in the hallways, give him the Jaguars growl. Grrrrrrrrrrr ..."

Ms. Kirkland jumped out of her seat. "Khalil, that's you?"

Khalil was so trapped in his own thoughts he hadn't even heard his name over the PA system.

"Me? What?"

"They said you were MVP for the team on the weekend. Congratulations! Good job. Everyone give Khalil, oh I mean Airplane, a hand."

Khalil lowered his head bashfully as the class rose to their feet, giving him a standing ovation.

"Th ... thanks, everybody. Thanks a lot," Khalil said, uncomfortable with all the attention. He turned to Cameron, who was clapping but with much less enthusiasm than the rest of the class, which Khalil thought was strange at first but didn't pay it any mind after.

"I didn't expect all of this," Khalil said to Cameron.

Cameron shrugged his shoulders and replied dryly, "Guess you're the new superstar." He sat back down without looking at Khalil. This reaction from Cameron was also something Khalil did not expect. He thought Cameron might have been happier for him. It was odd, but Khalil decided not to make a big deal out of it, figuring that Cameron was still upset about getting kicked out of the final game.

For the rest of the morning, whenever he had to change classes, Khalil was greeted with growls and high-fives. Everyone knew who he was and couldn't wait to interact with him, while Cameron seemed to be relegated to the position of sidekick. Completely opposite to how things normally were where Cameron was the most celebrated and Khalil was along for the ride.

CHAPTER 16

For the remainder of the day, Khalil could sense Cameron wasn't cool with the attention he was getting. Cameron was moody and snapped at him on the court during lunch when Khalil begged for a pass, yelling, "Don't tell me what to do!" As a result, Khalil decided to keep his distance during gym class the next period. Today was a joint class between their class and Dylan's and Blake's class.

Mr. Maracle was the gym teacher. Blake and Dylan's regular teacher had to leave suddenly, so Mr. Maracle took both classes for the period. As students filtered into the gym, Mr. Maracle asked them to take a seat on the floor. Normally Khalil would sit beside Cameron since they would walk in together, but today Khalil took his time getting to class answering questions about the basketball tournament from excited students. The other boys were already seated. Cameron and Blake were whispering and laughing with each other, so Khalil plopped down beside Dylan on the opposite side of Cameron and Blake. They greeted each other with a head nod as Mr. Maracle addressed the class.

"A couple quick announcements before we get class started. I'm taking Mrs. Sterger's class today so all of you will be working with my class. Also, many of you may know I'm the coach of the basketball team and we did well. Second place in the tournament on the weekend. We have a few of the boys from the team in this class, so everybody please give them a hand for their tremendous finish."

The class cheered and clapped, showing their appreciation for the boys.

"And not to single anyone out. They all played great, but Khalil over there won MVP honours for our team, so give it up!"

The cheers continued and got louder. One of the students began chanting, "Airplane! Airplane! Airplane!" and the rest of the class joined in. Mr. Maracle motioned for Khalil to stand. He did and quickly took a bow and waved at everyone. As he sat back down, Khalil looked in Cameron's direction and was surprised to see Cameron rolling his eyes. It felt like a punch to the gut when Khalil saw that. He would never guess that Cameron would react that way. Mr. Maracle quieted the class down before getting into his next topic.

"Okay, now I have something more serious to report. The staff was just advised about a terrible incident of racism in another Halton school. A school in Oakville. We were given this letter to communicate with our students. So, it says ...

"It has come to our attention that incidents of racist bullying and hate language being used by students and staff are inexplicably on the rise in Halton schools. This is something we will not stand for. We are taking measures to address and eliminate the use of hate or bias-motivated language in our institutions. Every student, regardless of colour, faith, heritage or orientation, deserves the opportunity to succeed in our schools without being victimized or feeling excluded. Every educator should be holding students to account, holding each other to account and holding colleagues to account for the language they use in the halls, in classrooms, in cafeterias and everywhere else. Every student needs to feel like they belong.

"We are aiming to eliminate the experiences of systemic racism for our Black and Indigenous students, which unfortunately have become more common. We will be strengthening sanctions for teachers who engage in behaviour of a racist nature, to ensure students feel accepted in a discrimination-free classroom. There will be zero tolerance for students who engage in racist behaviour, this includes racist bullying and hate or bias-motivated language. Mocking a student for their physical appearance, ethnic background, religious or cultural practices, even the way they talk or dress, will not be tolerated.

"We encourage students and staff to make incident reports with your school directly. Students, please tell your teachers or principal if you are involved in or witness an act of racist bullying amongst our students or staff. Your reports will be taken very seriously and we will be responding immediately to all incidents of racism and bias involving students and staff."

Khalil stared at the back of the page as Mr. Maracle read. He thought about the term zero-tolerance. *That means big trouble. Like being expelled. I would never do anything racist. I don't know anyone who's really racist,* he thought. The white page became a movie screen as Khalil remembered what Blake and Cameron said about Navdeep. Then he pictured the eyelid-pulling dance they did at Arnold Chen's house. The picture suddenly disappeared when Mr. Maracle lowered the page and began to speak.

"Okay, so I know that was a lot to digest, but it is very important. School should be a stress-free environment. All of you should feel free from ridicule and bullying of any kind. In the most recent cases, Indigenous and Black students have been under attack. I don't understand why. I mean, this hits close to home with me because it is students who look like my own children being victimized. Now, I don't believe that any of you have been involved in these attacks, but I do encourage you to come forth if you see anything, or especially if you feel you have been bullied in any way. Don't think that it doesn't matter. Or that the incident is too small. Trust me. We are taking every report of discrimination very seriously."

The class sat silently. They looked around at each other with faces that said, "I didn't do it. I didn't see anything."

"Okay, so you can take these handouts home to your parents. Put them in your book bags now, then meet back here and we'll get class started."

The students did as Mr. Maracle instructed. After class was finished, Mr. Maracle took Khalil aside as the other students headed to the change rooms.

"Khalil, I just wanted to say quickly that I am impressed with your progress this year. In such a short time, you've developed into probably our team's best basketball player, but not only that, the way you handle yourself now. Beginning of the school year, you were so introverted; I didn't think you were going to break out of your shell. Now I see you are so sociable. All the students seem to like you and it's good to see. I know this may not be applicable to you or this school, but if you do find yourself in a situation of prejudice or discrimination, you can talk to me. I'll make myself available. Okay?"

Khalil was caught off guard by Mr. Maracle's comment, but smiled genuinely and said, "Sure, Coach. Thanks. I think I'll be all right. No problems." Khalil left Mr. Maracle and headed to the change room, thinking how weird but also reassuring it was to hear that from Mr. Maracle. He pushed open the door to the change room and had to duck an object sailing towards his face.

The boys in the change room laughed aloud as Khalil playfully screamed, "Hey!! Watch out now. Don't hit this gorgeous face please puhleeeze. Hahahahaha."

Khalil located the spot near him where the object landed. It was a paper airplane.

"Whatever," Blake said, laughing. "Toss it back. Me and Cam are tryin' to finish our race."

Cameron had his airplane in hand, waiting for Khalil to fly Blake's plane back over. Khalil picked up Blake's plane, took aim and with a flick of the wrist floated it perfectly on target to the bench where Blake was sitting. Just as he let go of the paper plane, Khalil noticed some of the writing on the wing. Shocked, he walked closer to where Blake and Cameron were now standing preparing to let their planes fly and saw the same writing on the wings of Cameron's plane. Khalil didn't know what to say. He left the change room immediately in disbelief that the planes they were flying were made from Mr. Maracle's handout.

CHAPTER 17

Khalil hurried to the nearest washroom and changed out of his gym gear. His chest felt tight, and he had knots in his stomach. He debated with himself as to how Blake and Cameron could use the racism handout as an arts and craft toy. Did it not mean anything to them? He convinced himself it was only paper, and that they got the message during class, so perhaps it wasn't so bad of an offence. Khalil wondered if he was being overly sensitive and blowing it out of proportion. He was satisfied enough with this answer but still felt funny about the situation. In a way, he felt let down. Not by Blake so much, but he thought Cameron might see a connection between the racism warning on the paper airplane and the friend he called Airplane. Maybe Cameron just made the plane out of the nearest sheet of paper and hadn't thought about what was written on it.

That was good enough to release the tightness in his chest and loosen the knots in his belly. Although content with the excuses he made on Cameron's behalf, Khalil decided he would talk to him. Tell Cameron that the paper airplane wasn't a big deal, but maybe someone else might interpret it as if he didn't care about inclusion. That he might be unfairly pegged as prejudiced. Khalil rushed to his next class; coding class. He approached the entrance to the murmur of his classmates' chitchat, waiting for the teacher to begin. He saw Cameron already seated in his usual spot. Khalil walked over and sat beside him at his usual desk with a laptop.

"Hey," said Khalil as he took his seat.

"Yo," said Cameron.

They were silent as Khalil logged in to the computer.

"So where's your entourage? Didn't hear any growling when you walked in," Cameron said.

"Ah, man. I'll be happy not to hear another growl for the rest of the day."

Cameron smiled at that response. "Ya, it gets old pretty quick. Haha."

"Trust me!"

Khalil pondered if this might be a good time to bring up the paper airplane, but pushed the idea to the back of his thoughts.

"Hey, Cam. The real tournament is soon, right?"

"Ya dude. Like, week after next. We gotta make sure we're in top shape by then. We definitely gonna win Regionals, then go on to Provincials."

"We'll probably see Darcel again in Provincials."

Cameron's face went serious as he recalled the game they played against the Panthers.

"Ya. We'll show them. I got something for that point guard! Oh man, if we weren't at a school tournament I woulda given him these two biscuits ..." Cameron raised his fists. "... and a side of gravy."

Khalil and Cameron broke out laughing loud enough that other students peeked over and around their computer screens at them. Khalil considered that since things were light-hearted, now might be a good time to bring up the paper airplane, but Mr. Anderson rushed through the door.

"Sorry to keep you waiting, class. But I trust that you all have been prepping for today's lesson in my absence. Correct?"

"Coooorrect," most of the class replied with little enthusiasm while a few others responded with, "Yah. Sure."

"Excellent. So let's get right down to business. HTML Coding lesson five point two."

Mr. Anderson went through the lesson and then left the students to complete some of the coding exercises on their own. Khalil completed his quickly. He noticed Cameron was finished too because he was sending instant messages. Khalil decided he would just casually bring up the paper planes. As if it wasn't a big deal, but something he thought he should say. Khalil was sure this would be the best approach. That way, he wouldn't sound like he was condemning Cameron. He would just be making mention of it, from one friend to another. Like a heads up. Khalil was certain Cameron would understand and they could put it behind them promptly.

Khalil leaned over towards Cameron's computer. He had practiced his opening line in his head repeatedly and blurted it out, "Hey Cam. Those paper airplanes you were racing ... I'm sure it was just an oversight, but maybe the handout might not have been the best thing to use to make them. I mean, they looked cool, but like what if Mr. Maracle had seen them? You know what I'm saying ..."

Khalil hadn't realized Cameron's attention had been diverted to the computer next to him at the same time. Vanessa asked him to look at her work because she was having trouble with one of the coding exercises. Once Khalil saw Cameron was preoccupied, he took a deep breath and prepared to give his opening argument again when he noticed Cameron's computer screen. He unconsciously began reading the instant messages Cameron had written to Blake. Khalil's jaw dropped. His nostrils burned and eyes watered as he tried to digest what was on the screen. Khalil leaned back to his desk and sat up straight in his chair, staring at the ceiling. Cameron turned around shortly after and waved his hand in front of Khalil to get his attention.

"Yo, bro ... Airplane, wake up. Sorry, what were tryin to say?" Cameron leaned in close, whispering and snickering. "I think Van just wants me to sit closer to her more than really help her with her work. Hahahaha. Right!? Hahahaha ... y'know what I'm sayin'."

Khalil maintained the same position. He kept his eyes on the ceiling and the walls of the room. Cameron playfully jabbed Khalil's arm with his elbow.

"Yo, Airplane. You good? What's goin' on with you? You having a seizure or something?"

Khalil slowly raised his arm and pointed at the instant messages on Cameron's computer screen. Once Cameron realized what Khalil saw, he fumbled to quickly close the instant messages.

"Airplane. Yo, it's not what you think, bro. It's not what you're thinking. It's jus' talk. It's nothing."

Khalil sat quietly. Motionless. He was paralyzed.

CHAPTER 18

Khalil didn't say another word to Cameron for the remainder of the school day. He didn't even look in Cameron's direction until basketball practice after classes. The other boys had already made their way onto the court while Cameron waited until he and Khalil were the last ones left in the change room.

"Look Airplane, c'mon, I'm sorry you saw that. It wasn't meant for you. It's nothing. It doesn't mean nothing."

Khalil glared through Cameron, only seeing Cameron's instant message about the altercation with the Panthers' point guard appear before his eyes.

"You call that nothing!" Khalil said through clenched teeth. "Using the N-word is nothing! How am I really supposed to feel about that?"

"I was not talking about you. It was about that punk

point guard. I would never call you that." Cameron raised his palms in self-defence.

"You call those guys the N-word and I'm not supposed to be offended!"

"Well, ya. Well, no ... I wasn't talking about you. You're not one of them. You're different. We're friends," Cameron pleaded.

"A friend wouldn't do that. A friend would know better," Khalil said while shaking his head.

"I think you're taking this way too personally when I already told you it wasn't about you. If you didn't look at my screen, you wouldn't be upset now."

"What?!?" Khalil rolled his head back, glared at the ceiling, and breathed heavily.

"Ya, like you were reading my messages. None of this woulda happen if you weren't checking my screen," said Cameron.

"That's ridiculous. You are completely missing the point. Just get outta my way. We have practice." Khalil pushed past Cameron and entered the gym. Cameron sat in the change room for a moment before walking in. If the other players didn't know something was wrong with Khalil and Cameron before, they could sense it from their play on the court. Their usual bread and butter pick-and-rolls were out of synch. Khalil fumbled passes and threw up shots that clanked off the side of the backboard. Cameron's shot was off too, and he struggled to maintain control of the ball. After practice, Mr. Maracle stopped his two star players as the rest of the team made their exit.

"Hey, guys. Couldn't help but notice we were having a

tough time out there today. It's okay. It's just one day. Happens to all players. Tomorrow you guys will be back to form. At least I hope so," Mr. Maracle said, chuckling. The boys stared at him, blank-faced.

"Okay. Tough room," Mr. Maracle joked awkwardly. "You boys go get changed. Get some rest tonight. Tomorrow's a new day. Remember, we have the regional tournament next Friday, so we gotta have some of our best practices leading up to that day. Okay boys, see ya tomorrow."

Khalil and Cameron joined the others in the change room without speaking to one another. The only thing on Khalil's mind was getting home as quickly as possible.

* * *

The following day, Khalil didn't feel any better. He arrived at school, and for the first time in months, he didn't meet the other guys at the basketball court before classes began. He hung out in of front the school and then went straight to class once the bell rang. As Ms. Kirkland began her lesson, Cameron sprinted in and slid into his seat beside Khalil, who didn't even glance in Cameron's direction. Cameron's face was red and his hairline slick with sweat. It was clear he had been playing ball. Khalil could feel Cameron looking at him. Maybe he wanted to talk about the Raptors' win or make a joke about Ms. Kirkland's cold sore, but Khalil didn't look his way

Khalil watched Cameron through his peripherals. He didn't have anything to say to him and didn't want to hear a word from Cameron's mouth. Cameron's instant message kept flashing through Khalil's memory. It was the only thing he could concentrate on. He remembered wanting to talk to Cameron about the paper airplane and felt foolish thinking that folding up the racism handout was the worst thing Cameron was capable of. He wished it were. Mr. Maracle's voice echoed through his memory, "... if you do find yourself in a situation of prejudice or discrimination, you can talk to me ..." Khalil wanted to speak to someone, but it couldn't be the coach. That might mean trouble for the basketball team. He remembered what it said on the handout: "There will be zero-tolerance for students who engage in racist behaviour."

Khalil contemplated; could that be detention, suspension or worse; expulsion? He didn't want Cameron kicked out of school. He didn't even want him to have detention. Khalil just wanted Cameron to realize the effect what he wrote had on him and be at least remorseful and understand how hurtful that language was. Seeing Cameron punished wasn't going to give Khalil any satisfaction at all. He wondered if he could tell a teacher anonymously and not give Cameron's name. If he could do that, then he might feel better.

Khalil spent most of the school day ignoring Cameron and debating if he should tell and who he should tell about the Cameron incident. When it came time for basketball practice after school, Khalil still wasn't playing his best. He was not as off as the day before, but still was playing out of character. During a two-man chest passing drill where the boys had to give accurate bullet passes while shuffling their feet from baseline to baseline, he teamed him up with Navdeep, who noticed how out of character Khalil was throughout practice.

"Hey Airplane, you okay? Don't look like yourself, and to be brutally honest, I think I've been playing better than you today. And you're the star of the team."

Khalil shook his head. "Nothing. Just having a bad day. Happens to everyone. Don't sell yourself short. You've been playing pretty good lately, Nav."

"Thanks, man. But I know better. I'm not nearly the player you are. So something's really gotta be bothering you if you're playing like this."

Khalil thought for a moment before addressing what Navdeep said. "Okay, Nav, what would you do if someone you knew or like even say ... maybe someone on this team was using racist language. Not directly at you, about you or to you, but like ... if they said something about people in your culture in a discriminatory way?"

"You mean like if they said or called someone a Pak—"

"Ya, or even like the N-word, y'know, something like that."

"I think I would probably tell Coach."

"But what do you think would happen to that person?"

"Well, to start, they'd probably get kicked off the team ..."

Khalil's eyes widened. He hadn't thought about that possibility before. If Cameron was kicked off the team, they'd have little chance of winning the regional tournament next week.

Navdeep continued, "... then maybe they would get into some real trouble with the school board. Like didn't you hear about that one girl in elementary school who called another girl the N-word on the playground last month? She's been suspended indefinitely. Her parents have to keep attending arbitration meetings because they figure the parents are more to blame since she's so young. I think they'll let her back in school, but it will probably take some time."

Navdeep's face became serious and inquisitive. "So... who was it? Did someone on this team call you the N-word?"

Stunned by the question, Khalil quickly denied it. "No, no, no. I'm just talking hypothetically, y'know. I don't think anyone on our team would dare do that."

That moment Khalil remembered Blake and Cameron's reaction to Navdeep being chosen for the team above Blake. They had used racialized language about him, too. This had not been Cameron's first issue with race, and Khalil quickly grasped that this would likely not be his last.

"You sure?" Navdeep probed. "It would be a shame if you were protecting someone that maybe doesn't respect you enough not to use that type of language."

"Hey, we're up next! Let's go. Forget what I said. It's nothing," Khalil cut in, ignoring Navdeep's skeptical glare. Navdeep and Khalil completed their turn, then Coach Maracle advised the team to take a quick water break. Khalil was sipping from his water bottle when Navdeep approached him.

"Y'know Khalil, when I first moved to this area, I was riding my bike just around the corner from the school. Y'know just tryin to get familiar with the neighbourhood. And, umm. There was a car coming up from behind, real slow. Like in the movies before there's a drive-by shooting. So I was immediately suspicious. And lucky I was. Cuz as the car passed, a Slurpee cup came flying straight for my head. I ducked and red slushy splashed to the ground. The car was filled with boys yelling, 'Paki, you Paki. Get outta town.'"

"Holy smokes! So you never got hit? Did you see who did it?"

"That's just the thing. I couldn't really see who was driving, but the guys hanging out the windows with their middle fingers up looked a lot like Blake and Cameron. But I can't say for sure. The car sped away too quickly."

"Wow!" Khalil put both hands on top of his head.

"Ya, exactly. Wow, is right. So if you told me it was Cam using the N-word, I wouldn't be surprised."

Khalil looked away then adjusted his shirt as if it had been scratching his skin. "But have Cam, Blake or even Dylan done anything to you since that day? Did you ever ask them about it?" Khalil said.

"I don't need to ask those guys nothin'. I already know what they're all about. Blake and Cam are jerks. Dylan's not so bad, but he's soft. He just goes along with whatever those two are doin'. He would never stand up to them even if he knew what they were doin' was wrong!" said Navdeep.

Khalil stared blankly at Navdeep.

"I dunno Khal jus' ... just something for you to think about."

CHAPTER 19

The next morning at school, Khalil avoided playing the morning game. On his way to class, Dylan ran up to him. "Yo, Fighter Plane. You quit playin' wit us? You gonna play next break, right?"

"Hey man. We'll see. Trying to rest up for Regionals, y'know. Have this uhhh pain in my ankle." Khalil lied.

"Oh damn! Is it serious?"

"Nah, not that bad, just being cautious."

"Cool, okay, so you're gonna still play, right? We need you if we're gonna win. You and Cam. If you guys don't play good, then we're toast, bro. Got no chance."

"Ya, no worries. We're good. We're good," said Khalil.

"Alright, Planes Trains and Automobiles, catch you later, bro," Dylan said, holding out his fist.

Khalil dapped his fist. "Later," he said as Dylan began to

walk away. "Hey Dyl, wait a sec."

"Wassup?"

"Do you ummmm ... do you think Cameron is racist?"

"What! Why would you ask me that?"

"I mean, you hang out with him all the time, so if anyone would know, it would be you right?"

"You hang out with him, too. Probably more now than me. How could he be racist when you guys are good friends? If he was, you would know, wouldn't you?"

Khalil shuffled his feet uncomfortably. "I guess."

"I mean, sure, Cam may say some cruel things. But y'know he has a good heart, right?"

"But you've never heard him say anything racist before?"

"Cam ain't racist. Like, he says dumb stuff sometimes, but I don't believe he means half the stuff he says. I never take it personally. Neither should you. Y'know, that's just his personality."

Khalil shrugged his shoulders. Dylan jabbed Khalil playfully in the chest. "Don't worry so much, bro. We got a championship to win," Dylan said before heading to class. It was then that Khalil decided he wasn't going to say anything about the racialized language he saw. At least not yet, anyway. Not before Friday when they were going to play in the Regional tournament. He would give Cameron a chance to redeem himself, and if he continued with that type of behaviour, then he would talk to Mr. Maracle or another teacher.

As usual, Cameron rushed in just as class was beginning. He looked at Khalil. Khalil nodded. "Sup," he said.

Cameron was surprised, but instantly responded. "Sup, yo."

During class down-time, the boys talked as if the instant message never happened. They discussed where the Raptors were in the standings and what it would take to make another title run through the playoffs. They talked about the upcoming tournament and discussed strategies to make them come out winners for Provincials and even further. It was like old times. Joking around and having fun. Khalil had put all his feelings about Cameron's use of the N-word in a hidden place. Somewhere deep inside an emotional gunnysack, so he could still enjoy his friend's company without feeling guilty or totally at odds with himself.

As Ms. Kirkland dismissed the class for lunch, Cameron asked Khalil, "Hey you gonna play this break?"

"Uhhh, I think maybe I will. Ummm, I'll meet you guys out there."

"Yo, okay, don't take too long. I'll set up the teams," Cameron said as he jetted out of class.

Khalil wasn't completely sure if he was going to play. He wanted some time to think. He wondered if ignoring what Cameron had done was the right thing to do. It definitely made things easier. More comfortable for them both. Khalil ignored the nagging feeling that he should be doing something more about Cameron and made his way out to the court to meet up with the rest of the boys playing ball.

Khalil burst through the doors and ran out towards the group surrounding the rim. At first, he thought they were involved in an intense game when he heard all the shouting. Disagreements happened frequently when they played, so the noise wasn't alarming to Khalil until he got close enough to hear what was being said. A group of students who didn't normally play ball had circled all the players. They were yelling at Cameron.

"You're a racist. Just admit it."

"We know what you did. Don't lie."

It took a few seconds before Khalil understood what was going on. Navdeep was among the group that consisted of the other Brown and Black students in their grade.

"I don't know what you're talking about. Get outta here. We're tryna play!" yelled Cameron.

"We're not moving until you admit to it. We know you're the one."

"The one what!? You guys are crazy. I don't know what you're talking about."

"You're the one using the N-word. We know it's you."

Cameron noticed Khalil as he approached and addressed him immediately. "Hey, Airplane. Tell these guys I ain't racist. How can I be racist when me and Airplane are friends! Best friends. Where you guys getting that crap? Guh 'head Airplane, tell 'em."

Navdeep turned towards Khalil. "Ya Airplane. Guh 'head tell them. Tell them the truth. Guh 'head."

Khalil surveyed the faces of all the kids waiting for his response. He locked eyes with Navdeep, who raised his eyebrows, urging that Khalil reveal to everyone what he had told him earlier.

Khalil opened his mouth in protest. His tongue became dry. His throat burned as he declared, "He's not. He's not race ..." It was as if the words didn't want to be spoken. Khalil's voice turned raspy, then started to fade. He whispered the rest. "... cist. He's not racist."

The group wasn't convinced. Quintin, the strongest-looking one in the group, stood face to face with Cameron, breathing heavily.

"It bet' not be you. Better pray he's telling the truth. If we ever find out that you were the one, then ..." Quintin punched his palm as he spoke. "... then we will deal wid it. I guarantee you. We will handle it!"

Navdeep looked at Khalil with disappointment. As the rest of the group cleared the court, Navdeep spoke directly to Khalil for only him to hear. "You can't protect him forever. He's bound to do it again. Or worse, maybe he says it about you. Is that what you're waiting for?"

"So you come with an angry mob? Like what's that gonna do?"

"It's the only way guys like him will ever learn. That's what my older brothers do. They beat them down. Then they think twice about ever sayin' stuff like that again. A few bruises might do him some good, too."

Khalil looked to the ground as Navdeep's words penetrated the place he had stuffed all the emotions from Cameron's racist comments. He looked at Navdeep, shaking his head. "I never told you it was him. I never said anything."

"That's the problem. You didn't need to. It's written all over your face!"

Navdeep walked away, and the boys started their game.

The bell rang for class, and the players dispersed. On the way inside, Cameron grabbed Khalil by the arm.

CHAPTER 20

"Airplane. What did you tell those guys! Why they calling me a racist?"

"I didn't say nothing!" Khalil looked at Cameron with confusion.

"So why were they coming at me like that? You had to say something. What's your problem, yo? Are you tryin' to get me in trouble, get me beat down or something!"

Khalil looked around, wondering if Cameron was really accusing him. "No, I didn't tell no one."

"Whatever, Plane. Somebody did. You're the only one who could've." Cameron poked Khalil in the chest.

"What, are you mad at me?! I just saved your life, Cam. Quintin was going to knock you out. Probably I should've let him," Khalil said, knocking away Cameron's finger.

"Prolly you should keep your mouth shut. That's the

reason all of this is happening."

Khalil threw his hands in the air. He couldn't believe what he was hearing; that Cameron somehow thought this was all his fault. The knot in his stomach suddenly became tighter, and Khalil felt ill as he watched Cameron walk into class.

Khalil and Cameron didn't speak for the rest of the day. Both angry with the other. Khalil went home feeling horrible. He had a gut-wrenching discomfort that even his parents noticed and offered him ginger tea to help settle his stomach. If they knew the real reason for Khalil's stomach ache, their remedy may have included a trip to Khalil's school to speak with the principal and not just a home remedy.

Khalil didn't dare let his parents know. He felt embarrassed to even be in this situation. He thought it might reflect badly on him, so he didn't feel comfortable enough to share the issue with his parents. He knew immediately that they'd be furious.

Khalil went to bed that night, clutching his basketball for comfort. He lay on his back with the basketball in his right palm. He took a shot at a spot on the ceiling using perfect form, allowing the ball to roll off his fingertips and spin backwards until it nearly touched the kernels of his popcorn ceiling. He decided that if the ball landed back in his palm and the logo could be seen, then he would talk to Mr. Maracle about Cameron. But if the logo on the ball landed in his palm and couldn't be seen, he would just ignore everything as best he could. Khalil did this at least sixty-three times before dozing off and allowing his basketball to ricochet off his bed to the corner of the room after his last shot.

He woke the next morning to the one eye of his basketball staring back at him. He jumped out of bed to get ready for the game. That was the main thing on his mind. He wanted to win no matter what and wasn't about to let his distress with Cameron get in the way. That wasn't going to cloud his mind any longer.

Khalil arrived at school, checked into homeroom, then went straight to the lobby in front of the principal's office where Mr. Maracle instructed the team to meet. He was the first player there, and the bus hadn't yet arrived. Khalil peered into the principal's office in the direction of the secretary. He wasn't looking at her; he was recalling the game of heads or tails with the basketball he fell asleep to the night before. He had counted thirty-two for each argument before passing out. Khalil was snapped back to the present when the secretary waved at him. For a second, he thought he saw her motion for him to come into the office. Khalil froze and looked around to see who she was waving at. It was Mr. Maracle.

"Hey Khalil. You excited? You're the first one here. You must be ready to go."

"Well actually, Coach ..."

* * *

Khalil was the first to take his seat on the creaky bus. Mr. Maracle stood outside the doors as the team filed on. They were excited, talking loud, making jokes and predicting how many games they were going to win.

"Hey, Airplane! Where's Cam? He's not sick, is he?" said Stretch as he dragged his gym bag on the bus floor.

Khalil shrugged his shoulders and glared out the window before responding, "He's probably with Dylan. Don't think he's sick."

"Good! We need our dynamic duo to win this. Shake n' Bake. With you and Cam playing off each other, there's no one in this tournament who can beat us," Stretch said.

Khalil continued to stare at the window without saying anything. He was looking at his own image through the dirty glass. He looked into the bloodshot eyes of the boy in the reflection. He absorbed the troubled look on his face, the one he wore all morning and the night before. The boy in the glass didn't sleep well. The knot in his stomach was so tight last night that his face remained in a permanent grimace. If anyone was sick, Khalil thought, it was him. Sick of pretending, sick of the fake. Fakes are useful on the court, but in real life, he didn't want to keep up the charade. Khalil knew Cameron was wrong. What he wrote was wrong. What he and Blake said about Navdeep was wrong. The gestures he made about Arnold Cheung's grandmother were wrong. Khalil knew he had to do something about it, or the knot in his stomach would just keep getting tighter.

Last to step on the bus was Dylan, with a perplexed look on his face. He and Khalil stared at one another as he took the seat in front.

"Airplane. What's happening?" Dylan said.

Khalil shook his head, then continued to look at his reflection in the glass. Navdeep stood up, facing Dylan.

"Something that should've happened a long time ago."

"Whadayou mean?" Dylan protested.

"You can't shield him forever." Navdeep pointed to the group outside the front of the bus. "He's bound to get himself in trouble. And you too if you're not careful Dylan. You should at least know that."

"Who are you to judge, Nav?"

"I don't need to judge anyone. Especially when they expose who they are by themselves. You can't hide who you are, Dylan." Navdeep shrugged his shoulders and continued. "You just can't."

Dylan's attention went back to the door of the bus as Mr. Maracle, Vice-Principal Mr. Gouldbeck and Principal Mrs. Greene were speaking with Cameron. Mr. Maracle stepped onto the bus without Cameron. The whole team stared outside, wondering what was going on as the principal escorted Cameron back into the school and towards the office.

Mr. Maracle stood in the aisle of the bus to address the team. Khalil stared out the window at Cameron as the bus motored off. He already knew what Mr. Maracle was going to say. He knew exactly what was happening. As he watched the principal and vice-principal walk with Cameron, Khalil felt the knot in his stomach start to loosen. Khalil didn't feel much better, but he knew that by coming clean to Mr. Maracle this morning, he wasn't going to feel any worse.

ACKNOWLEDGEMENTS

Thank you to my family, my wife Nicolia and son Tyce. My sister Sheena and my parents Jemima and Listford Jones. Thank you for encouragement

Thanks to the BMBA: Brampton Minor Basketball Association, the first house league I ever played in and gained confidence as a player, then later gained confidence as coach. Thank you!

To the Milton Stags Basketball Club, thank you for allowing me to coach, to inspire and to be inspired by the youth who have played in the leagues.

To all the coaches I've had throughout my lifetime in every sport. Your energy and tutelage were invaluable to my development and to the values I now live by.

To my Knowledge Bookstore family, Sean and Carolette Liburd and Michele Liburd. Thank you for letting me live at your store (literally). Walking down from my apartment to access so many books about African culture and history has motivated my life incredibly. Thank you for the support of my artistic endeavors and for creating a space in Brampton where we could learn about ourselves and express ourselves.

Thanks to my brother from another and proofreader... Francis McLean and family: Julie Corona, Celia, Joaquin and Amina.